From Here to Timbuktu
A Steamfunk Adventure

By
Milton J. Davis

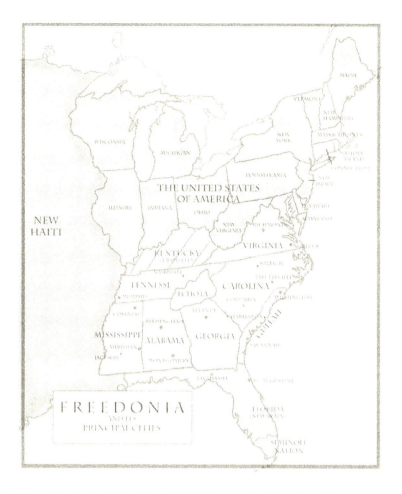

NEW HAITI

THE UNITED STATES
OF AMERICA

MAINE

VERMONT

NEW HAMPSHIRE

WISCONSIN

MICHIGAN

NEW YORK

MASSACHUSETTS

RHODE ISLAND

CONNECTICUT

PENNSYLVANIA

NEW JERSEY

ILLINOIS

INDIANA

OHIO

DELAWARE

MARYLAND

NEW VIRGINIA

RICHMOND

KENTUCKY

VIRGINIA

NORFOLK

TENNESSEE

TCHOTA

CAROLINA

MISSISSIPPI

ALABAMA

GEORGIA

GULAH

FREEDONIA
AND ITS
PRINCIPAL CITIES

FLORIDA
NEW SPAIN

SEMINOLE
NATION

OREGON

THE NATIONS

UNITED STATES
OF AMERICA

NEW HAITI

NEW SPAIN

FREEDONIA

FREEDONIA
AND ITS
SURROUNDING COUNTRIES

FLORIDA
NEW SPAIN

From Here to Timbuktu
A Steamfunk Adventure

By
Milton J. Davis

MVMEDIA, LLC

ISBN Number: 978-0-9960167-3-5
Cover art by Marcellus Shane Jackson
Maps by Sarah Macklin
Cover Design by Uraeus
Layout/Design by Uraeus
Edited by Rebecca Kyle

Manufactured in the United States of America

First Edition

To the Adventurer in us all

1

Five white camels crested the bright Sahara horizon, their blue robed riders swaying in time with their rapid gait. A score of men carrying ox skinned shields, metal spears and packs of various sizes followed, keeping pace as well as they could. The desert sun spilled its heat upon them, adding its burden on their weary backs. The riders did not care. The men were eklan, slaves, every one of them worth far less that the camels the warriors rode.

El Tellak, leader of the expedition, raised his hand and the riders slowed their pace. He pointed at a towering dune before them.

"This is it!" he shouted.

The riders urged their camels to increase their speed, expanding the gap between them and their servants. By the time the beleaguered slaves reached the foot of the dune the riders had dismounted. They were pacing before the sand mound when the first servant reached them. He approached them slowly, his tall frame and broad shoulders challenging the physical presence of his masters. Tellak struck the man across the face with an open hand.

"You're worthless, the lot of you!"

He marched away to his companions. The man he struck followed him with angry eyes.

"What are you waiting for?" he shouted. "Dig!"

The servant dropped his weapons then took a leather bag from his back. He opened the bag then extracted a folded spade.

With jerking movements he assembled the spade then marched to the dune. As he stabbed the sand his cohorts joined them. He watched El Tellak take a device from his saddle, a square box with a brass crank protruding from its side and a brass cone extending from the top. Tellak turned the crank rapidly for a minute the pressed his ear against the cone. After a few moments a voice crackled inside. He lifted his head then spoke into the cone.

"Yes, yes, we are here," Tellak answered in German. "The entrance should be clear soon. We will have the book before sunset."

He placed his ear against the cone again then nodded to the response. He looked at the other riders then shared thumbs up.

The punished servant eyebrows lifted when his shovel hit something hard. He dug faster; in moments a golden door handle appeared before him.

"We found it!" one of his fellow servants shouted.

The punished one said nothing. He continued digging until the door was completely clear. As the others ran to their masters hoping to be the first to share the news, the man turned the handle, opened the door then stepped inside. The innards of the buried temple were surprisingly cool. It was a circular room; its walls decorated with images that were not quite hieroglyphics yet not exactly paintings. The man recognized them; these were the symbols of a civilization which rose and fell long before the Great Pyramids cast their magnificent shadows across the Nile Valley. His eyes quickly found the prize; a large leather bound book resting on a marble pedestal incrusted with jewels. He hurried to the pedestal.

"What are you doing?"

The servant turned to see Tellak striding toward him, a whip in his hands.

"Worthless infidel! You're trying to steal from us!"

Tellak cracked the whip at the man. The servant extended his arm then watched as the leather wrapped around his forearm. In a sudden motion he jerked his arm toward his body as he extracted a dagger from his robes. Tellak, caught off guard, stumbled toward him then into the waiting blade. The servant wrapped his arm around Tellak, pulling him closer as he twisted the dagger. His former master slumped against him.

The servant dropped Tellak to the sand. He took a leather bag from under his robes then stuffed the book inside it. Securing it on his back, he made his way toward the temple entrance. The other slaves charged inside to confront him.

"This does not concern you," he said as he gestured with the bloody knife. "Stand aside or die."

His former cohorts quickly dispersed, hiding behind whatever they could inside the temple. When the man reached the entrance the other Ihaggaren waited on their camels, their takoubas drawn. The man secured the backpack then sprinted toward the Tuaregs.

The riders shouted before they kicked their camels forward. The man continued to run; when they were yards away he snatched two throwing knives from beneath his robes. The blades spun from his hands, one finding the face of a camel rider, the other the neck of a camel. The man fell from his saddle, dead before he met the sand. A second rider cried out as his camel keeled over. He attempted to roll free but the huge beast fell upon him, crushing him. The third man continued to attack, swinging his takouba over his head. The spirited servant continued running toward him, undeterred by the man and beast bearing down on him. At the last second he jumped to the left, a third throwing knife streaking from his hand then sinking into the head of the last Ihaggaren. The man gripped the knife as he tumbled from his camel onto the hot sand.

A strange sound from above signaled to the man that his dilemma was not over. He glanced up; a Prussian airship swooped down on him like a raptor, its shadow rolling over the undulating sand, its droning engine usurped by the chatter of Gatling guns. Bullets peppered the sand behind him as the man sprinted for the cover of a nearby dune. He dove as the bullets ripped the sand where he once stood. Reaching into his robes once again, he extracted two more throwing knives with thick handles. He hit the handles together and sparks flew, setting off a fuse in each knife. The man whispered a short prayer then stood, throwing the knives with each hand then ducking as the automatic guns fired. Searing pain flashed through his left shoulder and he grabbed it instinctively as his knives spun toward the airship. The blades bit into the airship's undercarriage, the fuses still burning. As the dirigible cruised over the warrior the knives exploded, setting off the flammable innards of the airship. The warrior ran for his life again, this time dodging falling bodies and flaming debris.

Once he cleared the burning deluge he checked his back pack then staggered to the nearest camel. He mounted the beast, ignoring his bleeding shoulder. The wound was painful but superficial; there would be time to bandage it later. For now he needed to put distance between him and the hidden temple. The book was secure; his task complete. With a jerk of the reins he turned the camel and set off for Timbuktu.

2

Deacon Ezekiel Culpepper strummed his guitar in time with the piano, trying his best to drown out Miss Parson's off key playing. The congregation sang as if nothing was amiss. Every year Reverend Pete promised the church he was going to replace her and every year he failed. The rumor was the Reverend was sweet on Miss Parson, but 'Zeke' knew different. A young girl up Atlanta way had the pastor's attention. It was Miss Parson's Sunday dinners that won her a place at the ivory keys.

After the final verse of Amazing Grace Zeke placed his guitar back in the worn case then took up a collection plate. He passed the brass plate to the thin, brown skinned coverall wearing man seated at the end of pew, sharing a friendly smile and nod. He repeated the gesture again and again as he worked his way toward the front of Piney Grove A.M.E. Church, collecting tithes for the latest service. The plate was heavy; Reverend Pete delivered a fine sermon full of fire and hope. Zeke lingered at one pew, staring into the pretty brown eyes of Pauline Rose.

"You lookin' fine today, Deacon Culpepper," she said.

"You, too, Miss Rose," he answered.

Reverend Pete cleared his throat, interrupting their brief moment of mutual admiration. Ezekiel finished the collection then passed the plate on to the other ushers. He strolled to the back of the church, nodding slightly at Miss Rose as he passed by. Reverend Pete blessed the offerings then delivered a hasty benediction. With that the congregation came to their feet, socializing as they slowly made their way to the church doors.

Ezekiel waited at the stairs, helping the ladies climb down. As usual, Pauline was the last to come. He held her hand as she descended then accompanied her to her wagon.

"You look like springtime in that dress, Miss Rose," he said.

"Hush up, Zeke. I wear this same dress every Sunday."

"Then it's spring every Sunday."

They stopped before Pauline's wagon. Zeke helped her up then checked the horse's bridle.

"I'm cooking a nice dinner today," she said. "Roast beef, snap beans, red rice and cornbread. Sure would be nice to share it with someone."

Zeke frowned. Spending the day with Pauline would be the perfect way to while away the time but he had things to tend to.

"I'd love to be that someone, but not today," he finally answered.

Pauline pouted. "Oh well. The invitation stands."

Zeke tipped his plantation hat. "I'll remember. You have a nice day, Pauline."

Zeke strolled to his horse with his hands in his pockets. He waited until Pauline was a good way down the road before mounting his horse then made his way to his farm. As he rode up the dirt path leading to his house he frowned at the unkempt fields and overgrown hedgerows. Zeke didn't have the time or skill to tend the farm nor the money to pay someone else to do it. Until he made enough to pay off the debt his parents left him things would have to stay the way they were.

As he neared the house he saw two familiar horses hitched to his post. He smiled; work had finally come his way. Sheriff Charley Wilson and Deputy Silas Moore waited on his porch. Sheriff Charley was a short round man with a moustache as big as his hat; Deputy Silas was a thin shifty fellow that never seemed to be completely still.

"Hey Zeke!" Charley called out.

"Hey Charley, Silas," Zeke shouted back. "What brings y'all out this way on a Sunday?"

"I got an urgent telegram from Marshall Stevens," Charley said. "Looks like the Bronner gang is heading this way. The Marshall wants us to keep a look out for 'em."

"What's the bounty?" Zeke asked.

"Twenty silvers," Charley replied.

Zeke dismounted then hitched his horse to the post. "That's good pay. When he expecting them to get up this way?"

"About three days from now."

Zeke walked up onto the porch and shook both men hands.

"What are they wanted for?" Zeke asked.

"Looks like they stole a book from a museum in Charleston," Charley replied.

Zeke pushed back his hat. "Is that all?"

"That's the most recent," Charley said. "They got a long list of charges, from murder to kidnapping. You bring them in you get the ransom for them all."

"That's more like it," Zeke said. "You bring the paperwork?"

Charley reached into his vest then pulled out the papers. Zeke took them and then flipped to the last sheet. There was no reason for him to read them; they looked just like any other bounty contract except the bounty was different.

"Got a pencil?" he asked Charley.

"Right here." Charley took a pencil from his top shirt pocket then handed it to Zeke. Zeke signed the contract then handed the papers back to the sheriff.

"Give me a week," he said.

"How you know it won't take longer?" Silas spoke up. "You don't even know where they are."

"If Zeke says he'll have them in a week, they'll be in our jail in a week," Charley said to Silas.

"Either that or dead," Zeke said solemnly.

The sheriff shrugged. "Don't make any difference. The pay don't change."

Charley and Silas tipped their hats as they headed to their horses.

"Sorry to interrupt your Sunday," Charley said. "Have a good day now."

"Y'all, too," Zeke answered.

Zeke waited until both men were beyond the gate before going inside. His house was a simple affair; one big room that served as sitting room, dining room and kitchen then a smaller room that served as his bedroom. He hung his coat on the rack by the door then went to the gun cabinet in his bedroom. He took out his Henry and his lever action shotgun then went back outside through the front door. With both guns under his right arm he took the reins of his horse into his left hand then sauntered around back to the dilapidated stables. After settling his horse he entered the barn. The building was filled with all types of guns, from muskets to bolt action rifles. A medium sized table occupied the center, littered with gun parts and various size bullets and shells surrounding a brass reloader. Zeke cleared a space around the reloader then pulled up a box of empty shells, shot and gunpowder. He rolled up his sleeves then picked up a shell.

"Lord, you know what I'm about to do. I just hope you understand."

Zeke's eyes narrowed as he began building bullets.

3

Field Marshall Dolph Eriksson crumbled the report with his gloved hands then threw it across the room. He swiped a stray lock of red hair from his prominent forehead then focused his hard green eyes on the captain that delivered the report. His look was as cold as the snow falling by his office window.

"Failure is unacceptable!" he shouted. "Unacceptable!"

The captain cleared his throat. "Unexpected circumstances impeded our plan. It seems one of Tellak's slaves stole the book after it was retrieved."

Eriksson looked at the captain. "These natives are an untrustworthy lot. There should have been contingencies. We should have been present."

"It was unavoidable, Herr Field Marshall," the captain replied. "Tellak has not failed us before. Besides, he wouldn't reveal the location of the book until he was prepared to exchange it. He feared we would not honor our debt."

"Who does he think we are, British?" Eriksson said. "Prussians always honor our word."

"They are natives, sir," the captain answered. "They don't differentiate between white men."

Eriksson pinched his chin. "What were our losses?"

The captain cleared his voice. "One airship and the entire crew."

"Shiesse!"

"And Tellak?" Eriksson required.

"Dead," the captain answered. "He was the first killed."

Eriksson waved his hand. "Leave me."

The captain saluted, turned on his heels then marched from Eriksson's office.

Eriksson slammed his fist on his desk. He'd have to file a report with his superiors; there was no way he could hide the loss of an airship. That meant he would have to endure another humiliating discussion about the importance of this mission. The captain said the natives were ignorant but as far as Eriksson was concerned he need look no further than the Second Reich for his fill of stupidity. Before Eriksson chose a military career he was an intellectual prodigy destined for a prosperous career as a professor at Ruprecht-Karls-Universität Heidelberg. But the family profession beckoned; that and the fact that military service in Prussia was mandatory. The man who excelled in academics also shone in warfare, becoming one of the main builders of the new German army that crushed the French so easily in the recent war. Like his family, he was a man whose bulk matched his brain; tall, broad-shouldered and thick armed.

Eriksson pushed away from his desk then strode to his window to gaze on the Arc de Triomphe. Winter in Paris should have been a relaxing time, but not this year. He was part of the Prussian occupation army that had come to make sure France paid its debt after losing the war. He came so he could distance himself from the Reichstag and pursue his project in peace. But the loss of an airship would require an explanation and he didn't have time to suffer ignorant people, not with so much at stake. He returned to his desk then took a piece of paper from his stationary. Dipping his quill into the inkwell, he composed a letter that he hoped would satisfy his superiors. Writing soothed his anger as it always did, allowing his mind to refocus on the business at hand. They would find the stolen book, of that he was sure. In the meantime his agents had informed him there was another book hidden in plain sight. That book was located in the most unlikely of places; Freedonia.

4

The desert sun rested low on the undulating horizon, dusky shadows extending across the sandy valley like the fingers of the Sau; the giants some say once inhabited the land. The current inhabitants of Kel Tellak, the new dwellers of the valley, were far from giants in stature but much taller in reputation. Feared by throughout the Sahel, known for their ferocity and ruthlessness, they were a direct reflection of their Akedamel, the Ihaggaren known as El Tellak, 'The Dagger.'

Dusk was the time for the evening meal, a game or two of oware and the gentle sound of the asak drifting through the kel. But this evening was one of a serious mood. Tellak's entire kel held vigil outside his tent. The senior women gathered about the entrance, their rhythmic chanting echoing off the nearby peaks. Behind them sat Tellak's family; his brothers, sisters, aunts, uncles and cousins. They chanted as well, although their cadence was frequently broken by tears and cries of anguish. Beyond them stood his warriors, each man draped in indigo robes, silent like the surrounding mountains. Their takoubas, cradled in their leather baldrics, hung from their shoulders; they held their allarhs and spears at their sides. Beyond them was the remainder of the kel, eklans and others who served Tellak. Their faces revealed a mix of emotions, some worried, some hopeful and some expectant. The chanting continued through most of the night but no one strayed. It had been a long time since El Tellak was wounded, a longer time since he'd been close to death.

Some gathered to pray for him; others to see him die.

Tellak cracked open his eyes expecting to see the judgmental glares of the ancestors. To his relief he gazed into Lemtuna's gentle face. He felt a cool towel on his forehead then a warm kiss on his cheek.

"You have returned," she whispered.

"You know I can't die," he said.

"You can and you almost did," she replied. He watched her as she checked the goatskin bag containing the serum. A thin tube ran from the suspended bag to his leg, entering him through a vein behind his knee. Despite the elixir he felt dangerously weak.

"Who did this to you?" Lemtuna asked.

"The Songhai eklan," he said, bitterness slipping into his voice.

"The new one?"

Tellak nodded.

"I knew there was something strange about him," Lemtuna said. "He seemed too eager to please for someone who just lost his freedom."

"He will pay for this," Tellak promised.

"I'm sure he will. Your sister hunts for him now. But you must rest."

She sat beside him, wiping his forehead again.

"What is it?" he asked.

She hesitated before answering. "It's the serum. It's taking longer to heal you."

"Then change the formula," he replied.

"It's not that simple," she said. "You know this. It's not only that. You have to take more now. The residual effect is not lasting as long."

"What are you saying?" he asked.

"You're developing immunity to the serum. Soon it won't help you."

"How soon?"

"I don't know. Next week, a decade, I'm not certain. But it will happen. Now is the time for you to seriously consider stepping down."

"No," he said. "There's still much to do."

"Menna is capable," Lemtuna said. "And she is anxious."

El Tellak scowled at his wife. "Don't speak to me of Menna. She will never rule the kel as long as I'm alive."

"I won't argue with you, Tel. Not today. But we will discuss this later. You can be sure of it."

Tellak closed his eyes as he smiled. Lemtuna worried too much. As strength seeped back into his body her warning took on less meaning. He was strong and would remain so until his task was complete. For untold years the Ihaggaren roamed Tinariwen as separate kels, fighting each other as much as they battled the surrounding Soninke, Berbers, Arabs, Bambara and others. But he was determined to make his people an empire that spanned the length of the Sahel. God had given him the strength, skill and Lemtuna's serum. His growing alliance with the Prussians was a great help as well, although that relationship might sour with the loss the book. He would have to rectify the situation.

Tellak struggled to sit up as the tent flap was swept aside. Two women entered, the older woman covered in indigo, her tasurwart embellished with jewels and beads. The younger woman was dressed in a simple green dress but heavily armed. Daggers belts crisscrossed her upper torso, an elaborate baldric containing an ivory hilted takouba hanging from her shoulder. The woman were related, the younger woman's face a reflection of her elder. Both frowned at Lemtuna before turning their attention to him.

"Mother, sister," he said.

His mother came to his side.

"Are you recovered?" she asked.

Tellak struggled to sit up. "I'm better."

"There is no more time," she replied. "Your people have waited long enough. They are beginning to doubt your strength."

"Some are hoping you don't emerge," his sister added.

"I don't need to hear the obvious, Menna," he replied.

Lemtuna stood opposite his mother.

"He needs a few more minutes."

"Be quiet girl!" his mother said. "No one speaks to you."

"But I speak to you," Lemtuna retorted.

The women glowered at each other. Tellak saw Menna's right hand grip her takouba hilt, her eyes on Lemtuna. He cleared his throat to get her attention; their eyes met then she released the hilt.

"I wouldn't expect you to understand what is at stake here since you are not one of us," his mother finally said. "This is a critical moment."

Lemtuna opened her mouth to protest but Tellak raised his hand.

"Mama is right, as always," he said. His acknowledgement of his mother's wisdom made her smile and gave her the victory she sought over his wife.

"Give me something," he said to Lemtuna.

"You will feel worse once it wears off," she warned.

"So be it," he said. "They need only to see me for a moment. Once they know I am restored they will leave knowing El Tellak still rules."

Lemtuna rummaged through her herb box then returned with a small white pill and a cup of water. Tellak took the pill then washed it down with a gulp; a wave of artificial energy rushed through his body. His heart beat hard against his chest as he stood. His mother nodded in approval then walked to the tent flap. Tellak followed, Menna close to his side.

"Did you find him?" he whispered.

"No," Menna whispered back. "But I know who he is and I know who he belongs to."

"That's not enough," he replied.

"I'll leave at daybreak," she said.

"You'll leave tonight," El Tellak said. "Don't return unless you have him."

Silence sat heavy between him. Menna was his sister, but there was no love between him. Five years ago she challenged him for leadership of the kel. It was a bloody, brutal battle which he barely won. Their wounds were so grave that Lemtuna was sent for to heal them. He was sure she would challenged him again if it wasn't for the serum Lemtuna administered to him. But she would be obedient for now, which was all he could ask.

"You have my word, El Tellak," Menna finally said.

Tellak grinned. He would have his revenge, if Menna didn't claim it first. Either way, the false slave would die by Tuareg hands.

5

The Elders were informed of Famara Keita's arrival earlier that day. They assembled in their chamber expecting his presence, the cool interior in contrast to the stifling heat of the dry season. Famara entered the meeting room to see them in a circle, eight men and women sitting on intricate blankets being served tea by attentive servants. Two horros accompanied him, warriors trained from childhood to serve the Elders and execute their plans. The bandages covering his shoulder wound hid under his robes; the book he'd been sent to retrieve in his hands. His fellow warriors led him into the center of the circle, proud smiles on their black faces.

Famara eased to his knees then extended the book.

"Elders, I have returned with what you seek," he said.

One of the elders, a short wide man with a thick gray beard stood then waddled to Famara. He took the book from Famara's hand then carried it to a woman wrapped in a colorful dress with large gold earrings hanging from her extended lobes. He opened the book before her; she took a pair of elaborate brass goggles from her sleeve then scanned the pages.

"Is it authentic, Kassaye?"

Elder Kassaye took her time studying the tome. After a few minutes she lifted her head, a smile on her face.

"It is as he says Yefarma," she confirmed.

The other elders nodded simultaneously. The squat man closed the book then walked away into the darkness.

"You have done well, Famara," the woman said.

"Thank you, aunt," he replied.

Another elder spoke, a man with the broad shoulders of a former warrior.

"What of El Tellak?" he asked.

Famara suppressed a grin. "Tellak is dead by my hand, Elder Bosso. May the vultures choke on his putrid flesh."

The elder nodded his approval.

Elder Yefarma spoke again. "For two years you sought this book. We are impressed by your dedication. You are a true horro."

Famara said nothing, his face warm with pride.

Yefarma closed his eyes. "It is because of this that we must burden you with another task."

Famara stiffened. He'd only been back days, barely enough time to enjoy the company of his wife.

"We know this is difficult for you, but this task requires your special skill. Besides, most of your task is complete. We know where the book is. Your job is to retrieve it."

If the location of the book was known his assignment would be much shorter. If the elders required his 'special skills' it meant his task would send him beyond the Sahel.

"I am here to serve you, elders," he finally answered.

"The book is in Fredonia, in the city of Atlanta," Yefarma said.

Famara nodded. "I will leave immediately."

"The ancestors are with you," the elder said.

"Thank you," Famara said.

He prostrated before the elders then left the chamber.

Famara stepped into the noonday heat fighting to keep his emotions in check. He'd pledged his service to the Elders immediately after his initiation rites. It was an honor he had no intentions of rebuking. But he had no idea what turn his duties would take. The discovery of Wagadu changed everything.

He trudged to the market and bought a chicken for the

evening meal as well as sorghum and dried dates. A few moments later he arrived at his family compound, greeted by singing and laughing. Children gathered about his legs, boys and girls dressed in colorful tunics that scraped their ankles.

"Uncle, uncle!" they cried.

Famara reached into his bag, pulling out handfuls of dried dates. He distributed them among his nieces, nephews and cousins as he walked, giving away the last one before his home.

"Did you save one for me?"

Kande, Famara's wife, leaned against the door well, a flirty smile on her beautiful face.

"Only the best one," he answered, "although its sweetness is bitter compared to yours."

He handed her a ripe date. Kande took it from his hand then placed it slowly into her mouth. She moaned with pleasure as she slowly chewed it.

"For this I'll let you inside...the house."

They kissed then went inside. Famara placed the chicken and sorghum on the table beside yams Kande prepared for the evening meal. Kande inspected the fowl as she chewed her date.

"Are the elders satisfied?" she asked.

Famara ambled across the room. He picked up the metal poker beside the fireplace and coaxed the waning flames.

"Yes they are. So much so that they've given me another assignment."

Kande slammed her palm on the table and Famara winced.

"No!" she shouted. "You've been gone for two years, Fa. Two years! That is enough."

Famara took a deep breath. "You know I can't refuse them."

"Yes you can," Kande retorted.

The house was almost silent, the crackling fire echoing off the mud brick walls.

"I can't," he repeated.

Kande didn't answer. She prepared the meal while Famara tended his wounded shoulder. Normally Kande would assist him, but not this night. He understood her frustration, but she knew his obligations before they married. Still, in the four years of marriage they'd spent scant time together. Worst of all, they had no children.

Kande sat the bowls of stew on the table and they ate.

"So when do you leave?" Kande finally asked.

"In two weeks," he answered.

Kande slammed her spoon down.

"No one else can do this?"

Famara wiped his mouth. "I must go to Fredonia to retrieve...an item. I am the only horro who can speak English."

"And how long will you be gone this time? Two years? Three years? Ten?"

"I don't know," he confessed. "But it won't be as long as before. This time we know where the item is located."

Kande folded her arms across her chest. "The item. And you cannot tell me what this item is, an item so important that my husband is taken from me for years at time."

"You know I can't."

Kande stood. "I'm your wife. You should have no secrets from me."

Famara looked away. "This is different."

Kande tilted her head. "Is it?"

She was right, of course. If something were to happen to him she deserved to know why.

"Let's finish our meal, then I will tell you everything," he said.

She took his hand then pulled him to his feet.

"Our meal can wait. Come with me. We will share secrets."

She led him to the bed, sharing an expectant smile.

6

The well dressed crowd waited patiently on the docks for the riverboat easing up the Chattahoochee River. The men sported an array of expensive hats; top hats, bowlers and plantation hats floating over the throng like felt clouds. Intermingled with them were fancy flowered hats protecting their feminine companions from the harsh winter sunlight. The ladies' beautiful dresses splashed with the hues of summer gardens broke the monotone of the men's black suits and added gaiety to the scene. This was a well-heeled crowd, ready to lose their wealth to the games of chance waiting inside the approaching vessel. It was a common Saturday scene in Atlanta but not the place for a sharp-eyed deacon bounty hunter with a wanted poster hidden inside his worn jacket.

Zeke stood out like a dead fish on an empty table despite his nonchalant demeanor. But he wasn't the only one. Three white men in cheap suits caroused at the dock entrance, one of them clearly drunk and proud of it. The ladies clinging to their arms were obviously paid for, their gaudy make-up and immodest clothing a clear sign of their profession. They seemed unaffected by the side glances and disapproving frowns of the genteel folks surrounding them. Zeke reached into his jacket, taking a glance at the bounty papers.

"That's them," he whispered. "Guess my hunch was right."

The riverboat band launched into a lively tune as the gambling boat docked. The revelers filed onto the deck, their boisterous voices expressing their excitement. Zeke held back. He took his cross from inside his shirt, holding it between his fingers as he closed his eyes and prayed.

"Dear Lord, please protect me as I take care of business. I know the commandments say thou shall not kill, so I'll try my best not to. But if it comes down to it, better them than me. Amen."

He kissed the cross then tucked it back into his shirt. Patting himself to check his guns then taking a deep breath, he joined the crowd boarding the ship.

By the time he reached the main gambling room the Freedonian Queen was well on its way. The players and dealers passed chips between them, the dealers receiving more than they gave away. The roulette table clicked as it spun, the sound occasionally drowned out by shouts of joy or despair from the blackjack and poker tables, depending on the luck of the gambler. Zeke's journey ended at the bar before a burly bartender sporting a bicycle bar moustache.

"What'll you have, sir?" the bartender asked.

"Whiskey," Zeke answered.

The bartender poured up a shot as Zeke reached into his jacket, took out a cigar then lit it. The bartender frowned at the cheap smoke as he placed the shot glass on the bar. Zeke tossed the man a coin then took a sip. He hated the bitter spirits as much as he hated the cigar smoldering in his right hand, but he had to keep up appearances. He was on a gambling riverboat cruising up the Chattahoochee, the last place Reverend Pete or the congregation would expect to see the soft spoken young deacon. But his profession took him many unlikely places, the bowels of the Freedonian Queen among the tamest. Though the church gave solace to his soul it didn't pay his bills. So he did what he was good at then prayed every Sunday for the good Lord to understand and forgive him.

Zeke placed the empty shot glass on the bar as he focused on his targets. Keith Bronner looked as out of place as a goat at a wedding, but judging by the smile on his sun-kissed red face one would think otherwise. His straw blond hair cascaded from under his new top hat, resting on the shoulders of his just as new tuxedo jacket. Zeke chuckled; it's a wonder what a man will spend his money on when the money doesn't belong to him. The two men standing on either side of Bronner were just as ill placed with their drab russet suits, faded derbies, and suspicious eyes. They scanned the otherwise highbrow crowd, obviously not comfortable with their older brother's current choice of distraction.

Bronner planted a wet kiss on his paid companion's cheek.

"Go ahead honey, draw the next card!" he chortled.

The plump red-headed woman reached out with exaggerated gestures, pulling a card from the deck. She showed the card to Bonner and he flashed a wide gap toothed grin.

"Damn honey, you are good luck!"

He took the card then laid his hand on the table.

"Royal flush, gentlemen!"

The other players folded their hands and fled the table, a look of relief on their faces.

"Okay, so you won," Jebel said. "Can we go now?"

"Boy, in case you haven't noticed we're still on the river,"

Keith replied. "We got about another hour before we dock. I suggest you find something' -he winked at the red-head- 'or someone to do."

"I just want to get off this damn thing," Colin said. A sick expression ruled his narrow face and Zeke grinned. He'd never seen a man get seasick on a river.

"You know folks is lookin' for us," Colin said. "We should be lying...hey!"

Zeke turned away just at his eyes met Colin's. He touched his neck where his cross hung hidden from view.

"Lord forgive me for what I'm about to do," he whispered.

Colin stormed over to him as the bartender slipped away.

"Hey boy, don't I know you?" he said.

Zeke kept his back turned until he felt a calloused hand

grip his shoulder.

"I'm talking to..."

Zeke spun, smashing his elbow against the side of the man's head. He drew his revolver from beneath his long coat, and then kicked Colin in the gut. The man doubled over into Zeke's rising knee. The blow shattered his nose and sent him reeling backwards.

"It's Culpepper!" Jebel shouted.

Bronner jumped from his chair, spilling the red-head onto the wood floor. He ran for the door. Zeke raised his revolver but before he could fire Bronner's bloody nosed brother slapped the gun from his hand.

"I'm gonna kill you, boy!"

"Not if kill you first!" Zeke swung the lever action shotgun from under his coat and fired, blowing the man halfway to the poker table. Jebel started shooting wildly as he ran for the door behind Bronner; Zeke and everyone else flattened on the floor until shooting stopped. He jumped to his feet, running out of the room and down the hallway leading to the outside. Jebel turned then fired again, barely missing Zeke. The bounty hunter hesitated; people jammed the hallway and while he had no qualms about shooting a criminal, he wouldn't risk the lives of innocent folks.

Jebel burst through the door at the end of the hallway. Zeke charged out soon afterwards. When Zeke finally caught up Jebel was climbing the side, ready to jump into the cold waters of the Chattahoochee.

"Come on down, boy," Zeke urged. "We can do this peaceful like."

Jebel turned with his revolver raised. "Go to Hell, coon!"

Zeke fired, blowing Jebel off the railing.

"You first."

Zeke ran the rail. Jebel's body floated down the river; he saw Keith Bonner stroking furiously for the shore.

"Shit!" He tucked his shotgun into his jacket then jumped.

The cold water hit him like a fist and it took him a moment to get his bearings before his swan after Bronner. By the time he reached the riverbank Bonner was staggering toward a stand of mulberry trees. Zeke took off after him. Bronner was about to plunge into the trees when Zeke called out to him.

"I can take you back dead or alive, Bronner! Don't make no difference to me. I get paid either way."

"I ain't going back to Reidsville!" Bronner shouted back.

"Maybe they'll send you to Andersonville this time."

"Or maybe not," Bronner spun around, a derringer in his hand. Zeke shot first. The blast lifted Bronner off his feet. He landed in the mulberries.

Zeke sauntered up to the woods then sat down hard. He watched the riverboat steam away then looked about. He would have to carry Bronner's body to the nearest police station to get his reward. He sat for a moment longer then lifted the dead man to his shoulders. Man hunting was hard business, he thought. Maybe it was time he started preaching.

7

Menna lay on her belly, the warm sand causing her to sweat beneath her robes. She watched the farm through battered binoculars, observing the farmers as they ended the chores for the day. Her attention focused on one individual, a tall, broad-shouldered man who moved with a lion's grace and balance. He herded his goats into their pen then distributed grass for the animals to feast on during the night. Another man laid dying miles away, a man who screamed out the location of the farm she now observed.

He was a weak man, far weaker than she expected, especially for one who claimed to be one of the mysterious horro she'd gleaned so much information about over the past weeks. Two knives tore the truth from his trembling lips, two minor poisons that would only upset an Ihaggaren child's stomach.

The man stopped his chores, suddenly looking in her direction. For a moment Menna thought she'd been seen but shook away the possibility. She was well concealed and too far away for ordinary eyes. Still, it was possible his nyama was perception and warned him of his invisible observer. It made no difference. When the time was right she would steal into the farm and get the information she needed.

Menna was loyal to El Tellak, her brother and Akedamel. Despite nearly killing him when she challenged him for leadership she would do what she was told until the time came to challenge him again. He was much stronger with Lemtuna's potions, but

Menna had her own advantages. Were it not for the timely arrival of the Bambara alchemist she would be Akedamel. The serum Lemtuna administered to Tellak neutralized Menna's venomous concoctions, so she worked diligently to create new formulations. There was no other way. In the beginning she attempted to befriend Lemtuna, but her brother swayed the plain woman with his charm then married her. Her second notion was to kill her, but that would be too obvious and bring the wrath of her brother down on her before she was prepared. So her only alternative was to wait until her poisons were complete, which would take some time yet. Accepting this mission gave her the opportunity to test their effectiveness and so far the results were encouraging. Another test would begin very soon.

The man finally retired to his mud-brick home. Menna waited, nibbling on bread and sipping water as the night trickled by. The sound of hissing sand soothed her; the occasional cry of a desert fox reminding her of the life that filled the desert despite its barren appearance. Hours passed but still she waited. There was a certain time when all people succumbed completely to slumber, a time when even the most vigilant became vulnerable to the needs of the body. Her own body told her when that time was nigh. Menna eased a red handled dagger from her belt then made a small cut on her wrist. This knife's poison was a stimulant when given in small amounts, but could push the heart to a lethal pace if given at a full dose. The slight burn was immediately followed by an energy rush. Menna rose to her knees, scanning the farm one final time.

She placed the binoculars into her waist bag then skulked down the dune to the farm.

The goats rustled as she passed their pen and Menna stopped, crouching low then making a quick sweep of the farm. Seeing nothing, she crept toward the house.

"Who are you?" a deep voice asked.

Menna spun toward the voice as she threw a dagger. The man knocked the dagger aside with his saber, the ringing sound like a crack of thunder in the quiet night. They fought between the house and the goat pen, the man working his saber with impressive skill, Menna defending herself with two special daggers. She heard commotion behind her but stayed focus on the battle before her, so great was the horro's skill.

"Go to the desert!" he said.

Menna took advantage of the distraction. She lunged under the swinging saber, raking her daggers across the horro's chest. The effect was immediate. The horro stiffened, his saber falling from his paralyzed hand. Menna dropped her daggers then caught the falling man. She maneuvered him onto her shoulders then trotted away from the farm with her prize. She ran until she was a good distance away. The others might come after her once they overcame their fear so she had to work fast.

She dropped the man into the sand then ripped open his shirt. She took a black handled dagger from her belt then made a small incision over the horro's heart. His body relaxed then his eyes opened.

"Tell me what I need to know and this will be quick," Menna said. "There was a man who stole a book from El Tellak. What is his name?"

The horro did not reply. Menna took a blue handled knife from her belt then pricked the horro's neck. The horro stiffened again, this time in obvious pain.

"The name is all I ask," she whispered in a soothing voice. "Give me the name and I will free you."

The horro struggled with the pain then cried out.

"Famara! Famara Keita!"

Menna smiled then took a white dagger from her belt. She raised her arm then drove the blade into the horro's heart.

"You are free," she said.

8

Dolph paced outside his commander's office. How dare Hans interrupt his planning for this meeting? He had nothing to do with the occupation; his only reason in France was to oversee the collection of scientific information the Reich deemed valuable. It was his concession for being allowed to pursue the books.

The door swung open and a young ensign stepped into the hall. Dolph stood as the young man saluted.

"Herr Field Marshall, the generals will see you now."

Generals? Dolph thought. This was not the meeting he expected.

Dolph entered the room to a disturbing sight. His friend General Hans Backer sat behind his massive desk, a look of concern on his face. Dolph wasn't worried about Hans; he was an old family friend and the husband of his oldest sister. It was the two other generals that unnerved him. General Claus Reuters grinned at him like a wolf, twirling the end of his black moustache. There was no love lost between them; Reuters was an ignorant fool that owed his position to the war's attrition of better officers. The other general, an older man with a fading mane was General Lukas Himmler. An excellent warrior in his day, the elderly general's skills were fading like his hair. He was still well respected and a good man.

"Sirs," Dolph said. "This is unexpected."

"But long overdue," Reuters said.

"Be quiet, Claus" Hans said. "Field Marshall, your reports

says you lost an airship in Mali. Is that true?"

Dolph cleared his throat to hide his anger. "It's in the report, sir."

"An airship is an expensive thing," Himmler said. "When we lose one, it should be because of a worthwhile endeavor."

Dolph turned to Himmler. "Herr General, the mission on which the airship was involved was authorized by your department."

"If I had known it was used to search for one of you books, I would not have authorized its use," the general replied.

Dolph looked at his friend. "What exactly is going on here?"

Himmler sat straight then cleared his throat. "Dolph, your family has served our country with honor for generations. You have been a valuable asset to the Reich. Because of this we have indulged your idiosyncrasies. But the loss of an airship raises the attention of others that are not so tolerant."

"So what are you saying?" Dolph asked.

"What he is saying is that your little escapades are at an end," Claus said.

Dolph looked at Hans. "Is this true?"

Hans nodded. "I'm afraid so."

Dolph stomped his foot. "This is outrageous!"

"Be careful," Hans warned.

"These books contain information that can transform our country! With them in our possession we will dominate Europe and the world for generations to come!"

"You expect us to believe that a couple of dusty scrolls written by savages contain such information?" Claus laughed. "It's true what they say. You are mad."

Dolph started toward Claus. The general came to his feet, his fists at his side.

"Stop this nonsense at once!" Hans shouted. He rose from his seat then walked around his desk toward the door.

"Dolph, come with me," he said.

Dolph followed Hans out the door.

"What is going on, Hans? You told me..."

Hans raised his hand. "It's beyond me, Dolph. Claus raised a stink before high command and they listened. You shouldn't have lost the airship. Especially in Africa."

"Look, Hans. Get me a meeting with the high command. My research must continue."

"Not for now," Hans said. "I want you to take a leave of absence. Go home and spend time with your wife and those wonderful children of yours. Things will calm down in a few months and you can pick up where you left off."

"No!" Dolph shouted. "We mustn't waste time!"

Hans glared at Dolph. "This is not advice. It's an order. Go home. I expect you to be on a train to Prussia in two days. Do you understand?"

Dolph shook with anger. "I understand."

"Good. Now come back later today and say goodbye when you've calmed down."

Hans smiled then returned to his office, closing the door behind him. Dolph turned on his heels then stomped down the corridor. He had no intentions of going back to Prussia, not with his program at such a critical state. Spending the military's money had been convenient but he knew it would run out at some point. It was time he took the program private. Hopefully the leave of absence would give him enough time to retrieve the other books and continue his experiments. But first, he would contact his resources. There was still so much work to do.

He hurried back to his office. Locking the door, he sat at his desk then wrote a brief letter to his wife:

Dear Angelika,

How are you and the children? I know I have been away longer than I promise, but my work in Paris demands my constant presence. A situation has occurred that forces me to make

decisions that will be detrimental to my military career and possibly damaging to our family's reputation. Please realize that I do not make this decision lightly; I have thought long on this and come to the conclusion that this is the right course of action. Please do not share this with anyone, especially Hanna. I do not wish Hans to be implicated in my actions. Please kiss the children for me.
Yours forever,
Dolph.

    Dolph folded the letter then placed it in the envelope.
    "Gunther!" he called out.
    Gunther Schmidt, Dolph's timid ensign, peeked into the room.
    "Herr Field Marshall?"
    "Come in, man," Dolph ordered. He handed the letter to Gunther.
    "Deliver this letter to my wife personally," Dolph said.
    Gunther's eyes widened. "Herr Field Marshall, shouldn't I use the postal service?"
    "No. I want you to hand this to my wife," Dolph said. "If anyone questions you tell them I gave you orders. You will be compensated."
    Gunther smiled. "Thank you, Herr Field Marshall."
    "I expect you to leave immediately."
    Gunther saluted. "Yes, Herr Field Marshall."
    The man scurried from the office. Dolph waited a moment then reached into his desk drawer, extracting the communication device built from the designs of the book in his possession.
    Those fools had no idea of the wonders contained on the pages of the books. He could have shown them, dazzled them with the communication box and astounded them with the other devices he'd constructed but now was not the time. He would suffer their ignorance a little longer, until the patents were in place and his factories were completed. Once his work was done he would reveal

his plans for the glory of Germany and his family.

He cranked the handle on the side of the box then pressed the sequence of keys.

"Herr Eriksson?" a familiar voice asked.

"Hello Tomas. Is Georg nearby?"

"No, sir, but I can contact him quickly."

"Good. Our plans have changed. Gather the equipment then meet me in Nice. We will proceed from there."

"Yes, Herr Erickson."

Dolph ceased cranking then sat down the talking box. He could be deterred, but he could not be denied. He would have the books, every last one, and no one was going to stop him.

9

The Malian airship gliding over Atlanta was a grand colorful sight, especially for a dreary, damp winter day. Its red and green striped body, dangling tassels and swirling Arabic lettering hinted at exotic intentions for the drab dressed Freedonians staring upward at its arrival. But the innards revealed a more mundane reality. The passengers were just as conventionally dressed as those below, a collection of various folk returning from business in Europe and Africa with a few returning Freedonian vacationers sprinkled among them.

Famara fidgeted in his first class seat, constantly adjusting his collar to hide his lower face. He looked about at the other passengers then tried to pull his collar higher. He realized what he was doing and he grinned. He'd been among the Tuaregs so long he felt exposed without a veil covering his face among strangers. He relaxed, looking about the cabin at his fellow passengers. He didn't expect to see anyone following him, but he was successful because he never took anything for granted. It was especially important that he didn't on this mission. His purpose was that important.

The airship eased into the mooring high above the main terminal. The landing crew tossed the docking ropes to the platform crew who secured the aircraft before extending the gateway. Famara took his satchel from below his seat then joined the shuffling procession to the exit door. The passengers nodded or tipped their hats absently to the lovely sepia skin woman welcoming them to

Atlanta, the jewel of Freedonia, as it was described. Famara looked into her eyes, imagining her with braided hair, her head covered by a royal blue wrap, large golden earrings and an amber necklace embracing her neck. He shook his head embarrassed; his missed Kande so much he was projecting her beauty on others. They spent their last days together making love, her desperation worrying him. He assured her he would return but in reality his fate was in the hands of the ancestors.

"Sir, are you okay?" the attendant asked.

"I'm fine," he replied. "I was...distracted."

She seemed to sense the meaning of his words. Her smile widened.

"I like your accent," she replied. "Where are you from?"

Her attention increased his embarrassment.

'Far away," he replied, and then rushed past her.

It was a long walk down the spiraling stairway which led into the bustling main terminal. Freedonia was a young vital nation and it showed in the confident attitude of its people. Its new president, Frederick Douglass, took full advantage of the peace that existed between the country and its neighbors after the short but bloody Reunion War. Many southern families that fled the region years ago in fear of retaliation from freed black laborers had returned to a land much changed from when the left, a country where prosperity touched everyone, not just a privileged few. Vice President Tubman worked diligently through her network of diplomats and spies to spread Freedonia's influence beyond North America, especially among the counties and kingdoms on the African continent. The Elders took note and were pleased.

After securing his baggage Famara worked his way though the crowd then stepped out into the damp chilly air. He marveled at the abundance of such a precious thing as water in this land. It was so different from his home, yet some things were too familiar. He took a moment to acclimate himself before setting off on the task given to him. First, he would locate the home of Pierre LaRue.

Second, he would secure a weapon. Third, he would take back what belonged to his people.

Famara studied the road signs at the intersection. He stood on the corner of Peachtree Street and Edgewood Street, precisely where the Elders instructed him to begin his journey. For a moment he stood motionless, acclimating himself to this new environment. He still was not used to men and women that resembled him in hue dressed similar to Europeans. But then they weren't like him. Their circumstances brought them to this land long ago; whatever they retained of their homeland hid under layers wool and cotton. Freedonia was young in terms of nations, born from the same fire of liberty that spawned the French and Haitian Revolutions.

Despite its youth Freedonia prospered and now it held an object in its possession that would increase its prestige even more. Famara planned to retrieve it before its value was discovered.

The streets bustled with horse drawn carriages, steam walkers and the occasional steam car hissing about here and there. He was familiar with the vehicles although he did not trust them. Once he visited Dahomey and was forced to ride in one of them. It was a most terrible experience; give him a good horse or better yet a camel and he could travel the world.

He reached inside his jacket then extracted an object which resembled a pocket watch but was much more. He studied it for a moment, the directions of the compass engraved on the golden cover in Arabic. He opened the cover revealing a single needle spinning furiously. He wound the device and the needle slowed. After a few more turns it stopped. Famara whispered a prayer then waited. The needle vibrated then turned to his left. As soon as it ceased whirling he felt a thumping in the palm of his hand. The compass watch was setting the pace at which he was to walk to arrive at his destination at the appointed time.

He followed needle's directions, turning here and there when prompted. A number of yellow steam cars pulled alongside him offering him a ride for a fee but he refused. No one needed to know his destination except him. Soon the busy avenues gave way to narrow quiet streets bordered by huge barren white oaks and concrete sidewalks. Majestic homes rested behind the trees, some of them gated, others open and inviting. Though they differed from the home of wealthy merchants of Djenne, Gao, and Zaria, their opulence was clear. These were the homes of those with wealth. He knew he was on track.

The compass watch ceased thumping. Famara beheld the house across the street from where he stood; an imposing red brick mansion built in French Provencal style. This was it, his destination. There was a large transport wagon parked before it. Two burly workers unloaded tables, chairs and other temporary furniture through the iron gates. If his information was correct, Mr. LaRue was having a party that night and Famara possessed a perfume scented invitation in his pocket insuring his participation. He now knew his destination. He took the compass watch from his pocket and rewound it. The needle pointed south and thumped out a faster pace. It was time he saw about gathering the other items he would need for the party.

10

Pierre LaRue paced the length of his opulent foyer, his wife Claudette watching in amusement. This was his debut into Atlanta society and he was nervous beyond belief. Ever since he fled the color caste restricted hierarchy of New Haiti for the true liberty of Freedonia he'd worked long and hard for this moment. His cocoa complexion wouldn't stand the scrutiny of Haitian high society, but in Freedonia he was truly among equals in every sense.

Claudette grabbed his arm as he passed by her for the eleventh time.

"Calm down, Pierre!" she urged. "It's just a party. Everyone coming knows you and loves you."

Claudette's beautiful smile eased his tension. She looked like an angel in her stunning gown. He sent her to Paris on a chartered airship to find it for he wanted everything to be perfect. He held her gloved hands in his then kissed her cinnamon cheeks.

"I know, I know mon cheri, but still I am nervous. You are used to such things. I'm just a carpenter's son."

Claudette cupped her hands around his cheeks. "You're more than a carpenter's son. You're an intelligent handsome man that I love very much. With the exception of your hair you look magnificent."

Pierre ran his hand over his processed mane. "This is all the rage in New Haiti!"

Claudette rolled her eyes. "When this is over I'm shaving

you bald myself."

Their laughter was interrupted by Horace, their butler. The tall stout man waited until they calmed.

"Monsieur et Madame, the guests are arriving."

"Thank you, Horace." Pierre said. The handsome couple inspected each other one last time before following Horace to the foyer then then taking their proper places. The two took a welcoming pose as Horace opened the grand door, greeting each couple and dignitary as they arrived with platitudes and smiles. Pierre's apprehension disappeared as he assumed the role of host. This was his forte, the innate talent that won over the New Haiti aristocracy and lifted him from obscurity to become the leading purveyor of fine furniture in the kingdom. Unfortunately no amount of money or prestige would open the doors of Haitian society to a man with such humble origins. Despite his marriage to Claudette Dubois, daughter of General Claude Dubois and confidante of the current king, Pierre was still refused recognition. His own father-in-law disdained him. He agreed to the marriage only because Claudette threatened to cut herself off from the family if not allowed.

Frustrated by his situation, Pierre brought his aristocratic wife and fortune to Freedonia in hopes of repeating his success. What he created exceeded even his grandest dreams.

Pierre was about to shake hands with Atlanta's Police Chief Martin Turnipseed when an arresting sight caught his eye. A man entered the door, a tall man whose head was covered in a red turban. Elegant robes cascaded from his broad shoulders to his fine leather boots. He held an invitation in his left hand, an elaborate wooden box in his right.

"My, my, who is this exotic guest?" asked the police chief's daughter. Mary Turnipseed was a tall, willowy woman who made up for her plain looks with an effervescent personality.

"I must admit I don't know," Pierre said.

Horace led the man to Pierre and Claudette.

"Monsieur and Madame, may I introduce Famara Kieta,

ambassador of Mali."

Pierre had to cover his mouth less he squealed with joy. Claudette's eyes widened.

"Bonsoir, Pierre and Claudette," Famara said. He shook Pierre's hand then kissed Claudette's. "Thank you for inviting me to your lovely home."

The couple looked at each other dumbfounded. Pierre didn't remember inviting any foreign dignitaries, but wasn't about to turn away such a pleasant surprise.

"Thank you for coming, ambassador," he finally said.

Famara raised his hand. "No formalities tonight. I am simply Famara."

"We're so happy you could join us," Claudette said. "You're French is perfect."

"We have some experience with the French in my country," Farama said. "Mostly bad."

Pierre hooted. "It seems Haitians and Malians have much in common."

Famara extended the box to Claudette. The surface was exquisite, festooned with intricate carvings. Pierre was impressed. Whoever did the work was a true master carver.

"A gift for the lady of the house," Famara said. "It's a special coffee from my homeland. I hope we can share it with your guests after dinner."

"Of course!" Pierre said. "Horace, take this to the kitchen and have it prepared immediately."

Pierre was beside himself the entire evening. The guests danced enthusiastically, and the only person that outshone his beautiful Claudette was the gregarious and handsome Famara. His stories of his country and the Sahel were riveting; the ambassador was the perfect segue way for Pierre's surprise.

After a few vigorous rounds of dancing the guests retired to the sitting parlor. Claudette touched Famara's hand for his attention.

"Farama, Timbuktu is located in Mali, is it not?" she asked.

The ambassador's eyes gleamed. "Yes it is."

Mary broke out in a giggle. "There's no such thing as Timbuktu!"

A look of dread came to Pierre's face. The silly woman was embarrassing. He expected an angry tirade from his guest but instead Farama smiled.

"As much as I hate to disagree with such a lovely woman, I must insist that Timbuktu is very real. I have visited many times. It lies not far from the banks of the Niger. It is an old and great city."

Mary's eyes widened. "Really?"

Farama moved closer to the naive debutante. "Yes, really. At one time it was the most important learning center in the world. Its libraries contain thousands of books."

Pierre's took advantage of Famara's statement. "Speaking of libraries, I have something to show you all that will confirm Farama's words."

He jumped from his seat. "Follow me please!"

Pierre led his small group to his library, picking up a few more curious guests along the way. They promenaded between towering shelves filled with leather bound books to a marble pedestal in the very back of the room. There, resting open was a book of obvious antiquity. Farama's attention was completely captured.

"Is this what I think it is?" he whispered.

"Yes it is, my new friend. This is a book from the library of Timbuktu!"

His guests gasped in unison. Claudette came to his side and clapped.

"Well done, my husband."

"You are a lucky man, indeed," Farama said as he continued to study the book. "How did you obtain it?"

"That I cannot share," Pierre replied. "All I can say is that nothing is beyond the grasp of money and determination."

Horace entered the room. "Excuse me, everyone. Dinner is served."

Pierre gestured toward the dining room. "Shall we?"

The guests followed Horace, with Pierre and Claudette leaving last. As they chatted and sauntered to dinner, Farama took one last look at the Timbuktu tome.

The dinner was an elaborate display of food and imagination. Again Pierre spared no expense, presenting a menu fit for every taste. The guest indulged in southern, Haitian and Creole cuisine washed down with the best wine France had to offer. For a moment he worried about Famara, but one glance at his Malian guest proved him in good hands. Ms. Turnipseed sat beside him, explaining every dish and practically putting the food in his mouth with her dainty hands. If the man wasn't careful he'd leave with a Freedonian wife.

After dinner they indulged in another round of dancing.

Mary grabbed Famara's hand then attempted to pull him toward the floor.

"Come, show me the dances of Mali," she said.

"I'm not a dancer," Famara replied. "My duties don't spare me much time for recreation."

Mary kept tugging. "Then I'll show you. I've been told I'm a good teacher."

Pierre stepped in, pulling Mary away and spinning her onto the floor.

"My God girl, don't be so forward!" he said. "It's unbecoming."

Mary stuck her tongue at him. "He's an ambassador and I've always wanted to travel."

"Patience, young lady," Pierre advised. "Patience."

The second round of dancing ended sooner than the first. Pierre led his guests to the parlor. The amazing aroma of Famara's coffee wafted throughout the house.

"If this coffee tastes half as good as it smells my life will be complete," Pierre remarked.

"It is very good coffee," Famara replied.

Martin Turnipseed finally spoke. "I thought Mali was mostly desert."

Famara nodded. "A large portion of our country is desert, however along the Joiliba, I'm sorry; the Niger River there is much fertile land."

The police chief still looked skeptical, but that was his way.
Horace and the other servants finally appeared with the coffee. They distributed cups and saucers among the guests then filled them with practiced precision.

Pierre took a sip and his mouth exploded with earthly pleasure. "My God this is outstanding!"

"Here, here!" Martin shouted in agreement.

Famara nodded.

"Horace, make sure you and the others have some of this exquisite brew as well."

Horace nodded. "Of course, monsieur." He and the other servants hurried back to the kitchen to indulge.

Claudette walked up to Pierre then, to his surprise, sat in his lap.

"This had got to be the best party I've ever attended! You've done a fabulous job, husband."

Pierre looked at his bride. Her lovely face blurred for a moment.

"Yes, yes I did." He shook his head but the blurring worsened. Claudette laid her head on his shoulder then he felt her full weight press against him.

"Mon cheri?" He lifted her slightly; she was fast asleep. Pierre craned his head around. The other guests were asleep as well, some stretched out on the floor. He tried to stand but dizziness pushed him back into his chair.

"What is going on?" he slurred. "What's happening?"

His eyes became heavy as lead. The last image he saw before sleeping was Famara leaving the parlor, heading in the direction of the library.

11

The congregation of Piney Grove A.M.E. Church emerged from the small white building single file into an unusually warm winter day. The clouds that harried the countryside with drizzle for two days had cleared, leaving the sky clear and the air crisp. Zeke walked the empty pews, making sure the parishioners left their seats clean and searched for any forgotten belongings. Reverend Pete had delivered another exceptional sermon, one that filled the church with energy and caused more than a few folks to get the Holy Ghost. He scanned the last pew then rested his hands on his waist.

"I guess that's it," he said.

"And none too soon."

Reverend Pete waddled down the aisle. He was as tall as Zeke but twice as wide, a victim of too many Sunday dinners at too many homes. He and Zeke had been friends since childhood. It was the reason Zeke was a member and a deacon.

"You better get on out there before Miss Rose loses patience."

Zeke smiled. "I don't know, Petey. Sometimes I think it might be better if she goes on home alone. I'm not the man she thinks I am."

Pete placed a hand on his shoulder and shook him. "I tried to tell her that but she won't listen."

Zeke gave Reverend Pete a mock scowl then they both

laughed.

"Well, I'm working on getting better," Zeke said.

Pete's face suddenly became serious. "Are you really, Zeke?"

Zeke took Pete's hand off his shoulder. "I'm here, ain't I?"

"Yes you are Zeke, but you ain't committed."

Zeke ran his hand over his head. "Don't start, Pete."

"Give it up, Zeke. Put the guns away and do what's right."

Zeke sat down. "You know I can't Petey. Mama and Daddy left me with a whole lot of land and a whole lot of debt. Ain't no way I can get a crop in the ground and sell it in time to make the next payment."

Pete rubbed his chin. "Must be another way."

Zeke stood. "Well, when you figure it out, let me know. I'm going to speak to Miss Rose now."

"Be a gentleman with that woman," Pete advised. "She's right fond of you. She could barely drink her communion wine trying to look at you."

Zeke grinned as he left the church. Miss Rose waited in her wagon under the bare persimmon tree, a smile as bright as day on her face.

"Well there you are!" she said. "I thought I was going to have to leave without speaking."

"How are you, Miss Rose?"

Pauline batted her pretty eyes. "Much better now. I have a fine supper prepared at my house just waiting for a man that looks just like you to come share it with me."

Zeke walked up to the wagon leaned against the buckboard.

"I'm not sure that's a good thing to do, Pauline. Knowing how we feel about each other we might find ourselves doing something sinful."

"You been talking to Reverend Pete again. I wish that man would stay out of our business." Pauline said. "Look, Zeke, I ain't no young girl. I'm willing to take that chance."

"I'll get my horse," Zeke said. He was about to head to the hitch post when he saw a familiar horse and rider lurking under the red oak a few yards away.

"Excuse me, Pauline. There's someone I need to talk to."

Zeke sauntered over to the finely dressed man.

"What the hell you doing here, Horace?"

Horace winced then rubbed his temples. "Not so loud, sir! Mr. LaRue sent me. He needs to see you immediately."

'I'll see him tomorrow," Zeke answered. "I'm about to take this young lady home for supper."

"It's very urgent," Horace said.

"If this wasn't holy ground I'd shoot you out of that saddle,"

Zeke said. "You know I don't conduct business on church grounds. Now you get on out of here and tell Pierre I'll see him first thing tomorrow morning and not a minute before. You got that?"

Fear filled Horace's eyes as he nodded. "Yes, monsieur. I do."

Horace spurred his horse and galloped away. Zeke shook his head as he went to retrieve his horse. Pierre must be in big trouble if he sent Horace to Piney Grove for him. But whatever he wanted could wait. Zeke liked the notion of Pierre afraid.

"Who was that?" Pauline asked.

"Business." Zeke tied his horse to the wagon then climbed in beside Pauline.

"Now let's go have some supper."

Pauline placed her hand on his thigh. "Yes, let's do that."

12

The sun slipped below the coastal Georgia horizon as the brass periscope broke the calm ocean surface. Helmut Kantor surveyed the marsh studded coast and surrounding waters for signs of any shrimpers, or worse still, Freedonian coastal frigates.

The Freedonian navy was a formidable force. Although he was certain they had never come across the likes of the submersible he commanded he could never be too sure. Freedonian technology matched the best Prussia had to offer, with a few surprises always in the wings. For that reason he spent a longer time than normal assuring their ascent would not be seen.

Three men dressed in tight fitting rubber suits stood behind him. Two of them, tall, blond men with wide shoulders and tight torsos, waited patiently. The third man, a broad built giant with red hair paced back and forth, his head barely clearing the pipes and instruments on the submersible's ceiling.

"Have you seen enough, Herr Capitan?" he growled.

"Not enough to my satisfaction, but apparently enough for yours, Herr Eriksson."

Dolph smacked his leg with his wide hand. "You do not grasp how important time is to this mission. We need to be on our way as soon as possible."

"You should have taken an airship," the captain replied. "It's much faster and it would land you in the center of Atlanta."

"You might as well tell me to saunter down Peachtree Street

leading a marching band!"

The captain faced Dolph with an unpleasant expression.

"Herr Eriksson. You hired me without explaining the purpose of your trip or the expediency of it. As a discreet person, I have refrained from asking you any details other than how much I will be paid and when. While I am tempted, at this point the question is irrelevant. We are where you wished to be. You can now leave my ship."

"It's about damn time!"

He turned to his cohorts. "Tomas, Georg, makes sure the crate is released."

The duo went about their duties. Dolph reached into suit and took out a leather wallet.

"Here is your second payment. You will receive the final payment when we return to Prussia."

"That was not the deal," Helmut commented.

"How else will I assure that you will be here when we return?" Dolph grinned.

Helmut nodded. "You have a point."

He snatched the wallet from Dolph's hand then turned to his sparse crew.

"Okay, take her up!"

By the time the submersible bobbed on the surface Dolph and his men were ready.

"Are you sure the location was confirmed?" Dolph asked Georg.

"Yes. Our contact sent us a message from Atlanta two weeks ago. Pierre LaRue definitely has the book."

"Good."

They opened the hatch and hurried across the submersible's cramped deck. The crate bobbed before them, released earlier through the waste tubes. Each man placed a mask over his face then jumped into the warm water. They swam in synch, secured the crate then stroked toward the marsh river before them. Once they reached the marsh they pushed the crate to the muddy bank then secured ropes to the exposed clasps. The box was more difficult to drag to the nearby road than Dolph anticipated; they were all exhausted by the time they reached the gravel roadway.

"Open it," Dolph ordered.

Tomas and Georg broke open the crate with crowbars. They reached inside then rolled out the contents, two kerosene powered motorbikes. With the motorbikes it would take two days to reach Atlanta, making the trip a total of four day. It was more than Dolph wanted to take, but it was necessary. The future depended on their success. His future most of all.

13

Famara led his horses off the main road into a thicket of pines and red oaks, following the throb of his compass watch. For the first time in his journey he doubted the device's instructions. He knew it contained the detailed plans of the Elders, but this detour made no sense to him. He had the book; now all he had to do was return home. But instead of the device guiding him to his planned destination it lead him to this desolate place.

Famara held no regrets of what he's done at Pierre's party. The coffee contained a heavy sedative; it would be hours before anyone revived and when they did they would suffer a severe headache. He remembered glaring at Pierre, his wife dozing in his lap, and he considered going to the man and slitting his throat. Instead he marshalled his emotions then continued his mission. When he reached the back of the library he looked on the book like a wounded soul. He took a leather satchel from his robe .then unwrapped a hidden corset from his torso. He assembled the corset into a rectangular box then set it beside the satchel. With extreme care he lifted the tome from its vulgar resting place, closed it, and then placed it into the satchel. Once in the satchel he placed the satchel into the box. He closed his robe then exited the library.

He shook his head in disappointment. The Freedonians were nice people, but they had no clue of the world around them despite their intelligence. Powers were at work that could change their lives forever, yet they danced as if they would be untouched.

He continued through the dense woods, dodging patches of sticker briers and blackberry vines bordering the narrow deer trails he traveled. His journey took him gradually uphill then steeped to a point that he and the horses had a difficult time gaining a foothold because of the slick piles of pine needles and leaves covering the ground. As they reached the hill's pinnacle the compass watch stopped pulsing. Famara took a moment to take in his surroundings. He was at the top of the steep pine tree infested mound with a panoramic view for miles. The road he abandoned earlier snaked through the brush, paralleling a broad muddy river.

The surrounding trees were thick enough to hide him but sparse enough for him to observe anyone approaching his position. How the Elders knew of such a place thousands of miles from his homeland puzzled him, but not for long. It was why they were Elders and he was a horro, a warrior in their service.

The horses wandered off to graze as Famara set up camp. It took him moments to gather wood then build a fire. He removed his iron cooking pot from his saddle bag then walked to the river to fetch water for his dried soup. After the brief meal he went back to his bag then removed the book from the satchel. Though he was certain it was the right book, he still had to inspect it. His original plan was to do so in the privacy of his room but the compass watch was insistent that he leave immediately, which he did. Now he had to conduct his test in the open, although there was little chance he'd be seen so far away from the city. He took another device from his bag, a narrow rectangular metal box with two terminals rising from the top and two bolts extending from either side. He set the box down then took out two handles which he attached to the bolts. Reaching into his robes he took out two cables, one green, and the other yellow. He attached the cables to the metal box then clamped them to the book. After mouthing a silent prayer, he turned the cranks as fast as he could. If this was a forgery the book would burst into flames. Instead the pages glowed. Famara smiled as the glow increased to a point where he could barely look at the book. Heat radiated from it like a roaring flame.

"By the ancestors!" Famara whispered.

He stopped cranking. The glow subsided, but the heat remained for quite some time. By the time it completely dissipated a cold darkness had settled over the landscape. Famara wrapped himself with a heavy blanket then stretched out on his back. It seemed he barely closed his eyes when he heard one of his horses snort. Famara continued to lay still as he watched two men creep into his camp. He suspected they were the two that followed him from Atlanta then pretended to ride off on a separate road. The fact that they scaled the hill after him meant their intentions were serious. Famara waited until the first man stood at his feet before pulling both legs to his chest then kicking out. The man's feet flew from under him. He crashed face first into the ground as Famara back rolled onto his feet. The other man had his revolver out and fired. Famara slipped to his left instinctively and the bullet furrowed his blanket. His revolver slipped into his hand from his sleeve and he shot the second man twice in the chest then shot the man on the ground in the head. He stepped over the first assailant, kneeling before him then removing his hat. The face was a clue to his origin, but he needed more. He opened the man's jacket and took out his blood-soaked wallet. The papers confirmed his assumption.

"Prussian," he said.

There was no time. He cleared camp as quick as he could. He had to return to Atlanta and get on the next airship out of Freedonia. Famara rode hard for the next hour until he reached the airship terminal on the outskirt of the city, its anchor towers blinking with red and white lights. His original plan was to travel overland to Savannah, giving time for his trail to grow cold. When he reached the port city his theft would be a bad memory. He would board a steamship to Whydah then join a caravan headed into the interior. His arrival in Djenne would go unnoticed except to a few trained to spot him and convey his return to the elders.

But everything changed with the Prussians on his trail. They were smart, ruthless and relentless. They also knew the value of the book. His hand went absently to the satchel strapped to his saddle. It was possible the city teemed with Prussian spies now, but the fastest way back to Mali was via airship. He would have to take the chance.

He kicked his mount then galloped into the city.

14

Zeke awoke to the smell of smoked sausage and scrambled eggs. He pulled aside the quilt covering his naked body then searched about the floor for his long johns. After putting them on and slipping on his pants he went to the kitchen. Pauline was setting the table, dressed in a white chemise. Zeke smiled as he admired her backside. She looked up at him and smiled back.

"Enjoying the view?" she said.

"Yes ma'am," Zeke replied.

Pauline shook her head. "I swear. You're definitely not a farmer. Here it is half past eight and you're just waking up."

Zeke rubbed his eyes. "Why are you up so early?"

"Cows don't milk themselves," she answered. "Got to get the eggs, too."

Zeke sat down before a plate of grits, eggs and sausage. "You did all that and cooked breakfast, too?"

"It's my routine." Pauline sat beside him with her own plate. "Don't see a need to break it just because a gentleman comes calling."

Zeke ate a mouthful of grits and moaned. He hadn't had grits so good since his mama passed away.

"If I was a gentleman I would have went home last night."

"You don't see me complaining, do you?"

Zeke leaned back and took a long look at Pauline. She came to Atlanta with her husband five years ago from South

Georgia. They bought the old Jenkins farm then settled in, Pauline working as a seamstress and Quinton, her husband, farming and making furniture. Quinton died from the flu three years later. Pauline continued alone, maintaining the farm and keeping up her seamstress business. She was a shapely woman with rich brown skin and a bright gap tooth smile that had men calling from miles around. But her only interest was for a man who was about as good a farmer as a door knob.

Pauline got up from the table and poured coffee for the both of them. She sauntered to the table then set down his cup.

"People are going to talk," Zeke said.

"People are going to talk no matter what," Pauline replied. "Might as well give them something good to talk about. Now drink your coffee. It's getting cold."

Zeke and Pauline finished breakfast then went back to the room and dressed.

"I'll chop a stack of wood before I leave," he said. "I owe you for breakfast."

Pauline gave him a sly grin. "You already paid for breakfast, dinner and supper. You get on about your business. I've got things handled here."

Zeke kissed her on the cheek. "You're some kind of woman, Pauline."

"You make sure you remember that Zeke Culpepper," she replied.

Zeke rode back to his farm. The homestead was a sorry sight compared to Pauline's immaculate spread; weeds crowding fallow fields, the barn barely standing. He didn't have the money to hire folks to repair it nor did he have the inclination to grow a single crop. Common sense said he should sell the land and be done with it, but it was all he had left of his parents. He entered his house, changed clothes then armed himself with his revolvers and shotgun. He didn't expect any trouble at LaRue's, but there was always a possibility of an altercation in Atlanta. A lot of folks did time in jail because of him and a few had scores to settle afterwards.

He also decided to take the steam car into town. His horse was tired and he was in a hurry. Besides, his winter driving coat hid his shotgun well. He took his horse to the barn, fed him fresh hay then pushed the vehicle outside. After a few minutes getting the boiler pressure just right he was on his way.

The ride to town was brief; the steam car was barely faster that his horse in a good gallop but handled the hills much better. Once in town he weaved around wagons, riders and potholes, occasionally yelling at pedestrians blocking his way as they stared at the vehicle. Steam cars were still rare enough in Atlanta to be a curious sight to most. The ride was smoother as he neared LaRue's home, the paved streets more favorable to his auto. What he saw as he pulled up to the mansion set him on edge. The front door was open, which wouldn't be unusual for a warm spring day or a cool summer night. But it was winter and chilly. Zeke parked the car then tucked the cross hanging from his neck into his shirt then took out his revolver. He crept up the walkway to the partially opened door. He pushed the door and it hesitated. He shoved it wider then peered in. Horace lay on his back, a gaping wound in his chest, lifeless eyes staring at the ceiling. It was then Zeke heard angry voices coming from the direction of the parlor. One voice was definitely LaRue's; his patios was unmistakable. The other Zeke didn't recognize. He took out his shotgun then worked his way toward the voices until he reached the parlor. He peeked inside to see LaRue sitting in a plush chair with two men standing before him, their weapons drawn. The third man held Claudette, a revolver pressed against her temple.

"Where is the book?" one of the men shouted. He was a tall, thick man whose face at the moment was as red as his hair.

"The damned Malian took it!" Pierre shouted back.

"He got here before us," the other man said.

"We'll have to find them." He then began speaking in another language, which meant they were about to do something they didn't want Pierre or Claudette to know.

"I didn't quite understand what you said," Zeke said, stepping out into the open.

"Shiesse!" one of the men shouted.

Zeke shot the man holding Claudette in the head. Claudette screamed then fell to the floor; Zeke dove for cover as the other two fired back. The shooting stopped; Zeke peeked out to see Pierre holding Claudette, her hair stained with blood. The men were gone.

Zeke ran back to the front of the house, rushing outside just in time to see the two interlopers speed by his steam car on motorbikes. He jumped in his car and gave chase, thankful he'd left the vehicle running. Despite his speed the men pulled away with each second. There was no way he was going to catch them so he turned around and headed back to Pierre's.

Pierre and Claudette were still sitting when he returned. Claudette jumped to her feet then ran to him, throwing her arms around him and smothering his cheeks with kisses.

"Thank God you came when you did! They were going to kill us!"

Pierre followed soon afterwards his hand extended. Zeke took it and was pulled into a grateful hug.

"Good timing man! Damn good timing!"

Zeke looked back at Horace's body. "Not good enough for Horace."

Pierre's other servants slowly filed out of the kitchen. When they saw the bodies they exploded in wails.

"Calm down everyone!" Pierre commanded. "Dante, go fetch the constables. Marie, take Madame Claudette into the kitchen and help her clean her hair. The rest of you go about your business the best you can."

The servants left the room, Claudette following Marie into the kitchen.

Zeke holstered his revolver then sat in the nearest chair.

"Looks like I'm on the clock," he commented. Pierre

nodded.

"We'll work out the details later," Zeke said. "My first question is who are these folks?"

Pierre shook his head." I don't know."

"Okay, my second question is, what did they want?"

Pierre's jaws clenched. 'That damned book!"

"All this for a book?" Zeke said.

Before Pierre could answer two servants reentered the room. They reached for Horace's body.

"Don't touch anything," Zeke said.

The servants halted then stepped away.

"You just want to leave him lying there?" Pierre asked. "He deserves more respect!"

"I don't think Horace is too much concerned about respect," Zeke replied. "I suspect he's answering for his sins right about now. Besides, the constables are going to want everything just like it happened so they can do the proper investigation."

"It's not right to leave him there," Pierre complained.

"We should follow Zeke's advice," Claudette said. She entered the room with a cooling towel pressed against her head accompanied Marie who scowled at Zeke. She sat beside her husband then sent the maid away. Marie glared at Zeke before leaving.

"You could have killed madam!" she shouted.

"Yeah, I could have, but those men would have. Why you think they started talking funny?"

"German," Claudette said. "They spoke German. I can't speak it, but I recognize it when I hear it. There were quite a few German students at Tuskegee when I attended."

"Was that some kind of German book?" Zeke asked.

"No, I was told it was from Africa, Timbuktu to be exact," Pierre answered.

"Who told you that?" Zeke asked.

"The men who sold it to me," Pierre replied. "The Bronner

Brothers."

Zeke pushed back his hat. "Well, they won't be telling anybody anything else anytime soon."

"Why?" Pierre asked.

Zeke shrugged. "So what would a bunch of Germans want with a book from Timbuktu?"

"I don't know," Pierre said. "I just want my book back!"

Zeke took off his hand then scratched his head. "Are you sure? Seem to me that Malian man may have done you a favor. Them Germans are going to kill him once they catch up with him."

"I want it back because it's mine!" Pierre shouted. "I paid good money for it!"

Claudette touched Pierre's arm. "Maybe he's right, Mon Cheri."

"There's only one reason you're here Zeke, and that's to get my book back." Pierre looked at Horace's body and a veil of sadness fell over his features. "Do whatever' -his eyes narrowed-'whatever you need to do to get it back."

"That might get expensive," Zeke warned.

"Don't worry. I'll pay."

They were interrupted by Marie.

"Monsieur, madam, the constables are here."

Ian McGinnis, West End ward sergeant, entered the parlor followed by two patrolmen. The constables wore matching navy blue uniforms with flared riding trousers and knee high boots, their gold button jackets crisscrossed with the shoulder straps supporting their billy clubs and revolvers. The patrolmen wore blue caps; Ian was bare-headed, his straw blond hair tossed about his head as if he'd been in a tussle. He nodded respectfully to Pierre and Claudette then shared a scowl with Zeke.

"I should have known you'd be here," he said.

"I only killed one of them," Zeke replied. "And I did that to save Madam LaRue."

Claudette nodded, confirming his words.

"Now that the authorities are here I best be getting about my work."

Zeke took a step toward the rear of the house when one of patrolmen blocked his exit.

"Not so fast, Culpepper," Ian said. "I may have a few questions for you."

Zeke gave the patrolman a hard stare. The patrolman swallowed then stepped aside.

Zeke looked over his shoulder at McGinnis. "You know where to find me."

Zeke left the mansion through the rear door. He figured since all the intruders to Pierre's home were from out of the country, the best place to look for answers would be the airship terminal. Even if they were long gone, he might find out where they went. And if Pierre was sincere about money being no object, he'd follow them to get the book back, even if it meant going to Timbuktu, wherever that was. He cranked up his steam car then headed to the terminal.

15

The Prussians weaved through the Atlanta streets to make sure they had lost their pursuer before heading to the airship terminal. Dolph gripped the handlebars of his motorbike so tight his knuckles paled. Whoever the man was that interrupted them would pay once the mission was complete. He glanced at his surviving cohort. Tomas nodded back to him. If Dolph had his way it would have been Tomas who was killed instead of Georg. Georg was a true asset, a multi-talented man. Tomas's specialty was killing and torture, two skills Dolph possessed as well. He looked at the metal box resting in the center of his bars. The street map of Atlanta scrolled before him, a brass arrow indicating his route.

Whoever took the book from LaRue could possibly still be in city. He assumed the perpetrator would head to the airship field for a quick getaway. Dolph signaled Tomas to follow him then wound his map box for a route to the terminal. The city map scrambled then transformed to the airship terminal route. The city buildings diminished until they sped across open fields and farmland; after riding for five more miles the Atlanta air terminal appeared over the horizon. Docking towers loomed over the large dome building, some awaiting ships, others occupied by dirigibles of various sizes and functions. A steady stream of customers paraded into and out of the terminal. It was a huge building, too large for Tomas and Dolph to search quickly.

Dolph guided his motorbike to the roadside. Tomas pulled

up beside him as he took off his gloves and goggles.

"We need help," Dolph said.

"From who?" Tomas asked. "We have few contacts in Freedonia."

Dolph grinned. "We don't need them. We have gold."

Tomas scowled. "You'll pay these people to help us?"

"We have no choice," Dolph said. "We'll go back to the city. I'm sure we'll find a few ruffians willing to help us find the Malian."

They rode their motorbikes back to the city. They cruised the streets, looking for a city section that existed everywhere, a place where everything and everyone were for sale. They smelled the city section before they saw it. It was the slaughterhouse district, the pong of death heavy in the cold air. A few blocks away was a row of drinking houses, each packed by hard working men and women eager to wash away the day's killing with hard liquor. The Prussians pulled up to the first tavern then entered. They were out of place among the dingy workers but didn't seem to notice or care as they strode directly to the bar. The bartender, a huge man with dusky brown skin and a balding head, spit as they approached.

"You're in the wrong place, pretty boys," he said. "Last thing these folks want to see at the end of the day is a couple of bosses trying to be sociable."

Dolph leaned into the man's face. "We're no bosses. I'm looking to hire a few men to find someone. You know of anyone looking to make a few extra eagles?"

The bartender scowled. "You ain't from around here, so I'll give you some advice. Get out on your feet while you can before you get dragged out on your backs."

Tomas tapped his shoulder. "Herr Eriksson, look!"

Dolph looked outside. A crowd had gathered around their motorbikes. One man was so bold as to sit on Dolph's, laughing as he pretended to ride. Dolph smirked. He tipped his hat to the bartender.

"Thank you for your help. I think I see the boys I'm looking for."

Dolph and Tomas strode to their bikes. The men turned to them, the one on the bike flashing a smile.

"Can I help y'all with something?" he said.

Dolph grinned back. "You're sitting on my motorbike."

The man laughed. "No sir, this is my motorbike...now."

Dolph laughed with them. He pulled out his machine pistol then shot the man in the head. Before the others could react Tomas had his gun out as well. The bartender stuck his head out of the door. He saw the dead man in the street then backed into the tavern.

Dolph put away his gun.

"Never underestimate anyone," he said. "But don't worry. I'm not angry with the rest of you. As a matter of fact, I have a business proposition."

The men looked confused. Some of them looked as if they wanted to run; others seemed interested in what he had to say. Finally a lanky man as tall as the bartender stepped forward.

"If you brave enough to shoot down Joe Diller and not haul ass you my kind of man. What you got?"

"I need to find a man," Dolph said. "And I need your help."

16

The Atlanta airship terminal consisted of a large dome structure with ten airship towers evenly spaced along its radius. Seven of the towers were dedicated to domestic ships; three to international flights. Because of the threat of plantationist infiltrators security about these towers was especially vigilant. Famara strode through the open terminal to the ticket window unconcerned.

There was no reason for him to be questioned or stopped; he would continue to use his cover as a diplomat to board the first ship out of Freedonia. It didn't matter where the ship headed; he would make it to Mali with the help of the compass watch. His priority for now was leaving the country before the Prussians discovered his whereabouts.

The conversation with the ticket master went smoothly. The amicable man directed him to Tower Eight, one of the three international towers. The first ship out was headed to England via a stop in New York. He walked briskly to the diplomatic gates, his hand gripped tightly to the satchel holding the book. He was almost to the gate when a wall of men appeared before him. The largest man, dark skinned with broad shoulders and a ragged grin stepped forward.

"We'll be taking that satchel from you, sir," he said.

Famara scanned the room as he lowered his head. These were not Prussians standing before him although he knew they were in their employ.

"I'm sorry. I can't allow that."

Famara kneed the man between the legs then smashed his elbow into his face as he fell. He spun under the grabbing arms of a second man then head-butted the third man in the face. He swept the fourth man's feet from under him then kicked him in the gut. He couldn't avoid the fifth man's punch so he rolled with it, diminishing its sting. He spun again, swinging his elbow to smash into the man's jaw. He was better than most; he ducked the elbow and tackled Famara. As they fell to the floor Famara lost his grip on the satchel. He raised his knees just before impact; the man crashed into them, air whooshing from his lungs. Famara flung the gasping man from atop him then sprang to his feet. The other men fled, one of them holding the satchel. Famara ran after them.

*　*　*

Zeke parked his steam car near the airship terminal stables.

He strolled into the building, heading directly to the ticket booths. Jason Killroy, an ivory skinned narrow man with receding hairline and ever-growing moustache smiled at him through the ticket booth bars and Zeke smiled back. Jason was a man always eager to make an extra eagle and Zeke always seemed to have a few.

"Zeke! How can I help you?" he said with a heavy Freedonia drawl. "Decided to take a flight?"

"I hate airships, you know that. I'm looking for somebody."

"A bounty?"

"Don't know yet. Anybody been through looking to go to Mali?"

Jason frowned while twisting the end of his moustache. "I don't think so. We don't have any ships heading to Mali. Now there was a man dressed kind of high and mighty in here. He bought a ticket to England."

Zeke slid five eagles to Jason. "Which tower?"

"That way. Just following those running men."

Zeke looked to his left. Four men hurried across the terminal, the first one carrying a brown satchel. Not long afterwards another man ran through. He was draped in a colorful robe that swished across the top of his boots as he ran, a red turban covering his head.

"Hey!" Jason exclaimed. "That's the man..."

Zeke was already running as he tucked his cross necklace into his shirt.

"I know."

* * *

Dolph and Tomas watched the hired ruffians run toward them, one with a satchel in his hands. They grinned at each other; this had been easier than planned. Their grin faded when they spotted the man pursuing the group.

"Gott in himmel!" Dolph's face paled. "A horro!"

Both men pulled out their machine pistols then aimed at the ruffians. The man with the satchel stopped, his face horrified as the Prussians began firing. The terminal erupted in screams and panic, people fleeing and falling to the ground for cover as the satchel carrier crumpled to the floor with five bullets in his chest.

The other miscreants fled in different directions, betrayed by their employers. The man with the satchel lay on his back, his upper body riddle with bullets from the rapid fire guns, his glassy eyes staring at the ceiling. The satchel handle was still gripped in his right hand.

"Get the satchel!" Dolph shouted to Tomas.

Tomas nodded then sprinted for the dead man. He was almost there when a fist smashed into his face, followed by another blow to his stomach. His eyes cleared long enough for him to see the horro's elbow aimed for his head. He raised his left hand to block the vicious blow to no avail. His hand smashed against his head and he fell to the floor unconscious.

Dolph sneered as he raised his pistol.

"Time to end this!"

* * *

Zeke witnessed the exchange between the robed man and the big Prussian. Whoever that man was he was a damn good fighter. In three blows he sent the hulking Prussian to the floor. The other Prussian drew a bead on the figure as he reached for the satchel.

"Now that just ain't fair," Zeke said.

He fired his revolver and the machine pistol flew from the Prussian's hand. The man turned to glare at him before diving for the floor then extracting another gun. Both men fired at each other; the Prussian rolling on the floor while Zeke shot back as he leaped for the safety of a nearby bench. He peeked out far enough to see the robed man running to the tower, the satchel in his hand. The wood over his head shattered from a barrage of bullets. Zeke crouched until the barrage ended then rolled into the open. The Prussian was running after the robed man.

Zeke loaded his gun.

"Pierre, I don't know what the hell you got me into, but there's about to be a mighty big up charge on my services!"

He climbed to his feet then chased the two men.

* * *

Famara weaved through the scattering crowd, running to the second international tower. If he was lucky the commotion in the station had not reached the towers and the airships were still departing on schedule. He dared to look back and saw the Prussian pursuing him, his machine pistol gripped in his hand. He turned away then crashed into a waiting constable, a tall thick man who wrapped his huge arms around Famara as the satchel flew from his hand. He watched helplessly as the satchel slid across the floor then came to rest against the leg of a startled woman.

"Now where are you going in such a hurry?" the grinning constable asked.

Famara answered with a head butt to the man's nose. The constable's head jerked back then he grinned, blood flowing from his nose.

"You call that a head butt?" The man jerked his head forward and Famara saw stars explode from the middle of his face.

He went limp and the man eased him to the floor.

"That wasn't so hard," the constable said. He was about to blow his whistle to summon his comrades when Famara swept his feet from under him. He fell flat on his back, his head smacking against the granite floor.

Famara staggered to his feet, his eyesight blurry. He stumbled about until he regained focus just in time to see the Prussian walk calmly into the third tower with the satchel in his possession. He reached into his sleeve for a throwing knife but thought better of it. There were too many innocents about. He took a deep breath then sprinted to the tower.

* * *

Zeke saw the dignitary defeat the burly constable. Every encounter made him more impressed. Whoever he was, he surely was no ambassador. He hoped when he caught up with him he could talk him into giving him the book. Otherwise he'd have to shoot him. Maybe not a killing shot, but something that will discourage him from using his hands and feet. The satchel was no longer in his possession; the Prussian had it, and he was entering the third international tower, the tower for airships to England. Whistles cut through the excited murmur of the crowd. The constables were coming in full force. Zeke picked up his pace, following the ambassador into the tower.

* * *

As soon as he entered the tower Dolph attacked the stairs, running at a pace that would impress the most disciplined athlete. He breathed at an even pace, his arms and legs pumping in perfect harmony. The stairs passed under his feet in a blur and he smiled.

There was no way the damned horro would catch him now. He was halfway up the stairs when he heard the ringing footfalls behind him. He looked down and grimaced.

"Shiesse!"

The horro was behind him and gaining fast. Dolph gritted his teeth and ran faster.

Zeke entered the tower staircase, expecting to see the ambassador only a few feet ahead. Instead the man was halfway up the stairway and closing in on the Prussian.

"I'll be damned!" Zeke took out his revolver. "This'll slow him down."

The stairwell exploded when he pulled the trigger. The ambassador disappeared but the Prussian kept running. Zeke tried to get set a good shot at the man but he's reached the top then exited the staircase. The ambassador appeared again, running much slower.

"Sorry, partner, but a job is a job." Zeke ran up the stairs.

* * *

Dolph stopped to catch his breath before entering the airship tunnel. He straightened his clothes then strolled to the cabin entrance. The concierge waited, a young freckled faced man with dull red hair. He looked at Dolph with suspicion.

"Welcome to British Air," he said. "Is there a problem? I seem to have heard gunfire."

"No, no," Dolph said. "I think some dropped a pipe or something. It made such a racket."

The smile returned to the concierge's face. "Your ticket please?"

Dolph handed the ticket to the man then took a quick glance behind him.

"Welcome aboard, sir. We'll leave momentarily. Enjoy your flight."

Dolph entered the luxurious cabin then took his seat. He looked to the door, expecting the horro to enter any minute.

The concierge appeared in the cabin, a megaphone pressed against his thin lips.

"Ladies and gentlemen, there seems to be some sort of disturbance in the terminal. Since this is a Freedonian matter and doesn't concern us we will take off immediately. Please take your seats, and thank you for flying British Air."

Dolph sank into his seat cushions and chuckled. He had the book and he was on his way home. Nothing could stop them now.

Famara limped up the stairs, his leg burning from the bullet graze. By the time he reached the top of the platform the airship was rising. He ran out onto the platform, tempted once more to reach for a throwing knife. Again he stopped. He had to retrieve the book intact. He was about to turn back when he saw the rope ladder dangling from the airship. Airship crews used the ladders to climb down to the platforms then secure the anchor ropes; apparently this ship departed in a hurry. He hobbled to the ladder, grasped the lowest rung and began climbing to the cabin.

Zeke burst onto the platform, revolver in hand. The airship drifted away with the ambassador climbing a stray rope ladder. Zeke paused for a moment to consider his options. He could walk away, give Pierre his money back and call it a day. He could shoot the ambassador for giving him such a hard time. Or he could jump on that ladder and get the book.

"Lord give me wings," he said. He ran as fast as he could then jumped, grabbing at the rungs. His right hand missed the bottom rung; Zeke experienced a brief moment of terror before his left hand snagged the next rung.

"Thank you, Jesus!" he shouted.

He steadied himself then climbed after the ambassador.

When he reached the top the bottom hatch was opened.

He stuck his head inside and was greeted by the barrel of an Enfield rifle.

"Come on in and join your mate," the gun wielder said with a deep Cockney accent.

Zeke climbed inside. Another man searched him, taking his revolvers.

"Two stowaways!" the rifleman said. "That's a record for Freedonia. Usually folks are breaking their necks to get into this place."

He clamped handcuffs on Zeke's wrists then marched him into the storage hold. The ambassador sat on the floor propped against a stack of crate. The airshipman shoved Zeke down next to the ambassador.

"We're too far out to turn around," the rifleman said. "You'll get your trip to England then we'll turn you over to the Freedonia Ambassador and send you right back home."

Zeke shrugged. There was nothing he could do for now. He looked at the ambassador and grinned.

"Sorry about your leg," he said.

The ambassador shifted suddenly. Zeke saw the elbow streaking toward his head, then darkness.

17

Zeke open his eyes to the sight of the ambassador's legs, his cheek wet with drool. He attempted to sit up but his head throbbed where the ambassador hit him. Normally he'd be angry, but he deserved it. He shot the man, after all. He lay still for a few more minutes then attempted to sit up again. This time he was successful. He shook his head clear then took stock of his situation.

He was handcuffed, sitting on the cabin floor, his back against a stack of supplies. The ambassador sat beside him, staring ahead as if entranced.

"Mighty good lick you gave me, ambassador" Zeke said. "I guess I deserved it, shooting you and all."

The ambassador slowly turned toward him.

"I'm no ambassador," he said in an unfamiliar accent. "You know this."

Zeke reached up and rubbed his head. "Yeah, I do. But since

I didn't know your name I chose to be polite. Better that calling you thief."

The man smirked. "I am Famara Keita."

Zeke nodded. "I'm Ezekiel Culpepper. Folks call me Zeke.

I hate to ruin the pleasantries, but I'm gonna need that book back you stole," Zeke said.

"It was your employer who stole the book," Famara countered. "I'm here to return it where it belongs."

"I don't care how Pierre came across that book," Zeke confessed. "Hell, I don't understand why anyone would want an old book that bad. But I was paid to bring it back and I intend to."

"Your friend Pierre is a fool!" Famara said. "He displays a treasure as if it is a trinket. If he knew half of what he possessed he would have never had it on display and I never would have had the chance to steal it."

"Like I said, Famara, I don't care. I'm doing the job I was paid to do."

Famara studied him for a moment. "What if I paid you more?"

Zeke laughed. "What if you did? Can't say I wouldn't be tempted. But looking at our situation I don't think you can."

"I can pay you three times what Pierre is offering if you help me get the book."

Zeke eyes went wide. "You don't even know what he's paying me."

"It doesn't matter. I could do this alone, but having someone else to assist will expedite matters. You have skill with weapons. That might be useful."

"If I agree, not saying that I will, what good will it do? We're locked up on our way to England to be turned over to the authorities."

Famara picked at his sleeve. "There are some who feel they are superior to others. When they let such feelings rule them, they then become weak, for they tend to underestimate their adversaries."

Zeke watched Famara remove a narrow piece of metal from the cuff of his sleeve. In seconds he unlocked his handcuffs. He rubbed his wrists then squatted before Zeke.

"Now my friend, how much must I offer you to assist me?"

"Thirty gold eagles," Zeke lied. His hand reached instinctively for his cross.

Famara gave him a wide grin. "You're lying of course, but

I'll pay it anyway."

He unlocked Zeke's cuffs.

"So seeing that you're an honest man, when do I get paid?"

Famara reached into his robe pocket then took out a fist full of gold eagles. He dropped them into Zeke's lap.

"I'll be damned, I mean....hell, I'll be damned!"

Zeke counted out the entire amount Famara promised. He gave 15 back to Famara.

"That's how I work. Half up front, the rest when the job's done."

Famara nodded. "I see we are both honest men."

Both men stood. Zeke searched about then found his guns. Famara returned with a shoulder bag.

"So what do we do now?" Zeke asked

"We wait until we reach London. The man on this ship, the Prussian, has friends there."

"Will we take him after he disembarks?"

"No. There is more to this than the book. We have to find out who else knows about it."

Zeke put on his hat. "Why all the fuss about this book? What's in it that's so special?"

Famara's face became serious. "The past, the present and the future."

They heard a door creak. They hid, Zeke taking out his gun. Famara shook his head. The airman came into view, Enfield in hand.

"What the bloody hell?"

Famara pounced from hiding. He wrapped the man in a choke hold and in seconds his arms fell limp as he sagged into Famara's arms. Zeke caught the rifle before it hit the floor; they dragged the man with them and waited.

"Ian? What are you doing in there?"

The second man entered and fell victim to Famara's hold.

"Are they dead?" Zeke asked.

"No, just unconscious."

Zeke pushed back the brim of his hat. "You got to teach me that."

Famara smiled. "Maybe I will."

They tied and gagged the two men then went to the port holes. London stretched out below them, its smokestacks and steam pipes fueling grey white clouds competing for sky with their natural brethren. The airship pilot positioned the craft over the platform.

Zeke and Farama disappeared among the cargo as ship workers appeared then lowered the rope ladders. Zeke was about to head for the door when Famara pulled him back.

"We'll wait until the ship is almost empty. People of our kind are not so numerous here. We'll be easy to spot."

"Our kind?"

Famara touched his skin and Zeke nodded in understanding.

"You're the boss," Zeke said.

The airship was secured and the passengers departed. The Prussian was one of the first to disembark. He was immediately approached by two men in black top coats and top hats who escorted him to a large luxury steam car. They sped away.

"So how do we find him?" Zeke asked

Famara reached into his robe and extracted his compass watch.

"Come. I'll show you."

18

"Famara Keita."

El Tellak paced inside his tent, his hands clasped behind his back. Lemtuna sat behind him, her narrow eyes shifting between her husband and his sister. Menna stood near the tent entrance; hand on her sword hilt as always.

"That is his name," Menna said. "He is part of a group of horro sworn to the Elders of Timbuktu. They call themselves the Sons of Gassire. What their purpose is I have not discovered, with the exception of the protection of the books."

"Why would they be so concerned with books?" El Tellak asked. "There are plenty of books in Timbuktu."

"Not like these," Menna replied. "These books are not from Timbuktu."

Lemtuna's eyes widened. "Not from Timbuktu? Then where are they from?"

"I don't know yet," Menna admitted.

"The books mean nothing to me," El Tellak said. "A book did not stab me, Famara Keita did. Where is he?"

Menna dropped her head. "I don't know. He is not in Timbuktu, nor is he nearby. It is suspected that the Elders have sent him abroad to retrieve another book."

El Tellak sat beside Lemtuna. "Keep me informed. In the meantime I'll contact the Prussians to see if they have any information."

Menna nodded then exited the tent.

"Those books are very important," Lemtuna said. "They may contain information that will help me modify my serum."

"How would you know?" El Tellak said. "You don't know anything about them."

"There are stories of cities that existed long before Khemet," she said. "Their knowledge surpassed anything we can imagine. This may be the source of these books."

"Like you said, these are stories," he said. "The desert is filled with the bones of men who chased stories."

"So why did you go hunting for that book for the Prussians?" Lemtuna asked.

"Because they paid me," he replied. "And I know the desert."

Lemtuna shrugged. "I think it's worth investigating. If not to confirm, at least to see if these books might help me...and you."

El Tellak gazed at his wife. "You have a point. I've let my anger obscure my reason. I will send more warriors to investigate."

"Why not let Menna do it? She has done well so far."

El Tellak laughed. "Menna probably has a trail of dead bodies in her wake. Sooner or later these horros will find out that she is hunting them and they will respond. The warriors I will send will be more discrete. Besides, I don't think we'll see Menna for some time."

"Why is that?"

"My sister knows where this Famara Keita is and she's going to kill him."

Lemtuna shook her head. "She would not lie to you."

"She always lies to me," he replied. "She won't give me the satisfaction of revenge."

Lemtuna shrugged. "Either way he'll die."

El Tellak smiled. "Or she will."

Menna listened to El Tellak and Lemtuna talk a few moments longer before slipping away. Her brother was wrong. She didn't know where this Famara Keita was located. But she would know soon.

19

Famara and Zeke melded into the arrivals. Both men ignored the stares from the other passengers and proceeded down the stairwell to the main terminal. They were halfway to the door when two stern faced men in blue uniforms and conical hats carrying short batons approached them.

"Police," Zeke muttered.

"They call them Bobbies here," Famara said. "Follow my lead."

"You're not allowed to carry those things," one of the said as he pointed at Zeke's guns.

"Pardon my servant," Famara answered. "He's very protective of me."

Zeke looked puzzled then looked back at the two men.

"And who are you?" the other man asked.

"I'm Famara Keita, ambassador to the Kingdom of Mali. This is my man servant, Ezekiel Culpepper."

One of the men lifted his hat with his club. "You're from Africa, then."

"Mali," Famara corrected.

"Mali, Africa, It's all the same to me." the man pointed his club at Zeke.

"This bloke ain't no African. He looks Freedonian to me."

Famara smiled. "He is. I find that Freedonians make the best servants. They have a history, you know."

The men laughed with Famara.

"How can we help you?"

"I'm looking for the nearest telegraph. I need to contact my consulate."

The shorter man pointed to a door across the terminal.

"You'll find it in there."

"Thank you for your help."

Famara and Zeke began to walk away. The taller policeman stopped them.

"You'll have to tuck those away," he said, pointing at Zeke's revolvers. Zeke took them off then stuffed them into Famara's bag.

He picked up the bag, following Famara's lead.

"Much better. Carry on, the two of you. And welcome to London."

The policemen strolled away.

"A history of service?" Zeke commented.

"I didn't lie, but I do apologize for the insult," Famara said.

"The British have little respect for our kind. You'll discover it soon enough. They especially don't care for Freedonians. You've caused quite a few problems for them."

Zeke shrugged. "Nothing they didn't bring on themselves. Who are we telegraphing?"

"The Elders. We need a place to stay."

They went to the telegraph service. The telegraph operator met them with a warm smile.

"How can I help you?"

"We need privacy," Famara said. He reached into his pocket then took out a handful of gold.

"That will buy you all the privacy in the Commonwealth!" the greedy eyed telegrapher said. He tipped his hat as he left the room. Famara worked the telegraph himself. After a few moments the reply came. Famara listened then opened the door, allowing the operator back in.

"Thank you," he said.

"Thank you, guvnor!" the operator replied.

Famara smiled at Zeke. "Our accommodations have been arranged. We're staying in the Langham Hotel. The Prussian is staying there as well."

"So we'll take the book back there," Zeke said.

"No," Famara replied. "The game has changed. There is a diplomatic ball tomorrow at the British Consulate General's office. We are on the list and so is the Prussian."

Zeke stopped walking. "Wait a minute. We're just going to walk up to the man and introduce ourselves?"

"You can introduce yourself," Famara replied. "He already knows me."

They walked out to the terminal and into London. The sights and smells of the capital of the Empire assaulted Zeke. The social distinctions were obvious; well-heeled men and women moving among the hordes of poor as if they were invisible. Large cumbersome steam mules plodded through the streets laden with cargo and supplies. Steam cars mingled with horse drawn carriages and pedestrians. He followed Famara to a man dressed in a black uniform and cap.

"How can I help you?" the man asked.

"We need transportation to Langham Hotel."

The man raised an eyebrow, shrugged his shoulders then blew a shrill whistle. Moments later a steam car chugged out of the darkness then up to the curb where they stood. Zeke opened the door for Famara and they both climbed in. The driver maneuvered through the crowded street then stopped before a majestic multi-story building with a grand marble entrance.

"The Langham," the driver announced.

They exited the car and Famara tipped the driver. Zeke looked the building up and down, visibly impressed.

"Well I'll be damned...I mean, this is something else. These Elders of yours must be pretty special."

Famara grinned. "You have no idea. Let's check into our

rooms. We have a banquet to prepare for."

The brown-skinned bellhops met Zeke and Famara at the curb. They hesitated at the sight of the two then glanced at each other. They looked back at the duo with grins on their faces.

Welcome to the Langham," they said in unison.

They led Famara and Zeke to the desk where they checked in amid a crowd of curious and disapproving stares. Famara did an excellent job at ignoring the attention; Zeke stared back with a disgruntled frown.

"These folks act like they've never seen black folks before," he argued.

"They've never seen black people checking in here," Famara replied. He handed Zeke a key.

"Take my bags," he commanded.

Zeke pushed back his hat. "Excuse me?"

"My bags. You're my manservant, remember?"

"Oh yeah, right." Zeke strolled to the bellhops. "I'll be taking those."

The bellhops shook their heads.

"No mate. It's our pleasure." The man who spoke extended his hand. "Tommy Branson's me name."

Zeke took his hand then gave it a hearty shake. "Zeke Culpepper. This here is Famara Keita, councilor of the kingdom of Mali. "

Famara nodded then Tommy tipped his hat. "It's not often we get dignitaries of your persuasion if you know what I mean. Follow us."

Zeke didn't argue. They followed the bellhops to the lift then ascended to the 5th floor. The bellhops led them to side by side suites.

"This is the ambassador's room," Tommy said. "Yours is next door. You gentlemen have a nice stay. We'll tell the staff to take special care of you."

"That's right nice of you," Zeke said.

Famara reached for his pouch to tip the men but they shook their heads.

"No need, guvnor," Tommy said. "Like I said, we're taking special care of you."

"There should be a change of clothes coming soon," Famara said.

"Meet me in the lobby in an hour. Bring your guns."

Zeke nodded then entered his room followed by one of the bellhops. The room was amazing, filled with antique furniture and a large rice bed with an elaborate canopy. He tipped his hat to the bellhop but the man lingered.

"Is there something else?" Zeke asked.

"No sir. I was just wondering if you were Freedonian."

"I am."

"God bless you, sir!" he said. "You Freedonians are giving the Empire what for."

Zeke tried to give the man a tip but he shook his head. The bellhop left the room and Zeke fell into the plush bed. He didn't have time to feel exhausted for as soon as his head touched the pillow he was asleep. An insistent tapping on his door finally woke him. He opened the door to a lovely housekeeper holding his tuxedo.

"Here you are, sir," she said with a knowing smile.

On any other day Zeke would invite her in, but he was on the job. He took the tuxedo and ushered the lady from his room. The tux fit perfectly; Zeke went to the lobby wondering how Famara's friends could have picked a fitted tux for him at such short notice. Famara stood in the lobby waiting, just as immaculately dressed.

"Where are you guns?" he asked.

Zeke patted under his arms. "I had a time working my holster right but I managed."

"Good. Let's go."

They exited the hotel. Famara took out the clock compass, gazing at it for a moment before walking off to the left.

"Now tell me again why we're going to this dance?" Zeke asked.

"I had a primary and a secondary task," Famara replied. "My primary task was to secure the book and bring it back to Timbuktu. I failed."

"I wouldn't say you've failed," Zeke said. "We're on his tail."

Famara looked at him scowling. "The Prussians have the book. This situation forces me to take on my secondary task."

"And that is?"

"Find out why the Prussians want the book so badly. I'm hoping that when the Prussian sees us he'll hasten to his destination. We'll follow him and discover his plans."

Zeke shifted his hat. "You actually think it's going to be that simple?"

Famara smiled. "No."

Famara halted before the theater, classical music escaping from its doors where the reception was being held. Zeke began walking to the entrance but Famara stopped him.

"Wait," he said.

They waited for thirty minutes before the door opened. A black man in a waiter's outfit exited. He approached them, his face serious.

"Follow me."

They trailed the taciturn waiter down a back alley behind the building to a rear entrance.

"This is our invitation?" Zeke asked.

Famara shrugged. "It's the best the Elders could do on short notice."

They entered through the kitchen, the staff eyeing them as they continued into the ballroom. A small symphony played a lively tune as finely dressed men and women spun and twirled across the floor. Most of the men were dressed in military uniforms.

"There he is," Famara said. He strode into the ballroom and

Zeke followed. The dancers stopped, staring at the intruders. A few of the military men walked toward them; Zeke opened his jacket, exposing his revolvers. By the time they reached the Prussian the room was silent.

Famara stood almost nose to nose with the man.

"I believe you have something that belongs to me," he said.

The man's face was flush, his hands balled into fists.

"I have no idea what you are talking about, African," he said through his teeth.

"Of course you do," Famara replied. "You could make this easy and turn it over now."

"I suggest you leave immediately," the man said. "The Prussians and British are friends. The authorities are on their way."

Famara nodded. "Until we meet again."

He turned and walked away. Zeke backed away, his jacket opened, then turned to follow Famara. They left the way they came.

"So that's it?" Zeke said.

Famara nodded. "He'll run now, and we'll follow."

They walked toward the end of the alley. Zeke saw a flash of light and his hands went instinctively for his guns.

"Hold up. There's..."

A loud grating noise filled the alley. A contraption entered the muted light, a machine resembling the mechanical mules they saw at the landing field. However this machine was designed for a different task. It towered over them on two legs, a massive Gatling in one robotic hand. The other hand was an elongated drill bit.

"Move!" Zeke shouted.

The alley exploded in light and gunfire.

Zeke shoved Famara toward the towering mechanical man. The cobblestone where they once stood was ripped apart by lead rounds, sparks lighting the alley behind them. The machine angled its head down then walked backwards, trying to catch its running targets. Zeke had no doubt he could reach the streets before the steam giant could get them. A childhood of chasing piglets and calves then running from bulls and stallions made him quick on his feet. He was happy to see that Famara was a quick stepper as well.

They darted between the brass legs, barreling for the alley opening when their escape route suddenly filled with British soldiers armed with rifles. Zeke's revolvers were in his hands before the Brits could take aim. He blasted off six rounds while shoving Famara back toward the mechanical man. The soldiers ran for cover while two of their cohorts crumpled to the ground.

Zeke and Famara made it to the automaton's legs. Above them, through the hissing steam and rattling gears they heard the angry voices of the men controlling the contraption.

"Where the hell are they?"

"I think they're under us!"

"Shit, we can't shoot them there!"

"Maybe the soldiers will get them."

"Fool, our own men might bloody well get us if they shoot!"

Zeke watched the end of the alleyway for any soldiers attempting to look inside. He felt Famara's hand on his shoulder.

"I'll be back," the Malian said. He reached into his tuxedo jacket, pulled out a wicked dagger, then proceeded to climb up the mechanical man's back.

The soldiers at the end of the alley saw his move. They rushed out into the open, aiming at his climbing companion.

"No hell you don't!" Zeke said. He released a deadly fusillade, taking down three more riflemen and sending the others back for cover. Moments later he heard clanging metal above him then the sounds of struggle. A body dropped in front of him, smashing into the cobblestone. A minute later another hit the stone behind him.

"Zeke, get up here!" Famara shouted.

Zeke holstered his guns then clambered up the back of the mechanical man, working his way around the belching steam engine.

When he reached the head a metal door swung open. He climbed inside; Famara sat in a stool before a control board peppered with gauges and levers. There was an empty stood beside him. A solitary lever rested in front of it.

"Get in," Famara said. "I'll drive. You shoot."

A wide grin spread across Zeke's face as he jumped into the gunner's seat. The mechanical man lurched forward under Famara's steering and they trudged toward the alley entrance. As soon as they emerged into the street Famara swung the unit left to right. Zeke followed with bursts from the Gatling gun, taking out the British troops. Famara steered the metal behemoth down the street toward their hotel.

"We'll stay inside for a few more blocks to make sure no one else follows," he shouted over the engine noise.

"Can we keep it?" Zeke shouted back.

Famara shook his head. "Of course not. Besides, they'll know we have it soon. If they built it, they know how to destroy it."

Famara maneuvered the machine into a wide alley. They climbed out then disabled it by cutting the hamstring cables and puncturing the water supply tanks. After peeking from the alley to make sure they hadn't been followed they hurried for the Langham. They turned the corner to the hotel and a discouraging sight greeted them. The hotel swarmed with Bobbies and British soldiers.

"What do we do now?" Zeke asked.

"Follow me," a voice said from behind. Both men spun, Zeke with revolvers in hand, Famara with his dagger.

The man raised his hands then illuminated his face with the candle he carried. It was one of the bellhops.

"When the bobbies came we figured it was for you,' the man said. "I figured they weren't going to let a couple of black blokes stay in such a fine place too long."

The man extended his hand. "I'm George Pinckney. I know who you two are."

Famara and Zeke shook his hands.

"Now come on with me. We'll hide you until things calm down."

"What about our things?" Famara asked.

"That's taken care of," George replied.

"Where are we going?" Zeke asked.

"The East End. It's not fancy, but you'll be safe. Besides, the Reverend wants to meet you."

Both men looked puzzled. George laughed.

"Don't worry, the Reverend's a friend. As a matter of fact, he's probably the only person that can get your arses out of this bloody mess."

George started down the road. "Follow me."

Famara and Zeke tucked their weapons away then followed George into the darkness.

20

The trio worked their way through the foggy night, in and out of narrow alleys and down empty streets until they reached the East End. Zeke and Famara were infuriated by what they saw. Ragged row houses lined narrow streets filled with those who couldn't afford a room in the dilapidated buildings. The stench was awful, heightened by the canals that served as sewers.

"This way," George motioned.

They followed him until they came to a narrow church with a battered steeple crowned with a broken cross. George motioned them to wait then he climbed the gritty stairs. He took out a ring of keys then unlocked the door. He waved them up and they entered the church.

The inside of the church was better than expected. They walked down the aisle between plain but sturdy pews then continued around the pulpit. Hidden behind the pulpit was a door that led into a small kitchen. A tiny table sat before a stove with a large pot simmering on top. A short stout woman was opening the lid when they entered.

"' 'ello mum!" George shouted.

The woman jumped, almost dropping the lid.

"What?" Her eyes narrowed when she spotted George.

"You almost scared me to death, boy!" She raised her spoon then lowered it when she saw Zeke and Famara.

"I'm sorry sirs," she said. "I didn't expect you so soon."

"No need to be sorry," Zeke said. "Whatever's in that pot sure smells good."

The woman grinned. "This ain't nothing but rice and beans."

"Beg your pardon, but we haven't had a thing to eat all day," Zeke said.

Famara nodded. "This is true."

"Well sit down then!"

George pulled out the chairs for them.

"I'll run get the Reverend while you eat."

They sat and the woman filled two pewter bowls with rice. Famara studied his for a moment but Zeke immediately gulped down a spoonful. His mouth was filled with fire and flavor.

"Ooh Wee!" he exclaimed. "This has got to be the best rice I've ever had!"

Famara finally tasted his. "Interesting."

They were eating when George returned with the Reverend. He was a dark-skinned tall man, bone thin with a beard that grazed his chest. His eyes lingered on Zeke for a moment then went to Famara. Both men began to stand but he waved them back to their seats.

"Welcome to the East End," he said with a Freedonian accent. "You two have been very busy."

Familiarity lit Zeke's face. "You one of Scofield's boys, ain't you?"

The Reverend smiled. "Yes I am, Ezekiel Culpepper."

Zeke's smile faded. It wasn't good for the Dispatch to know your name.

"Who is your friend?"

Famara stood then extended his hand. "Famara Keita, from Mali."

"Randolph Turnipseed," the Reverend said. "I'm glad you refrained from using that Malian ambassador cover. I know the ambassador very well."

Reverend Turnipseed leaned against the wall then folded his long arms across his chest.

"So who do you represent, and why are you agitating the Prussians?"

"I represent an organization with worldwide interests," Famara answered. "The Prussians have something that belongs to us.'

"And that is?"

Famara smiled. "A book."

"A book Pierre once owned," Zeke chimed in.

"So that's how you became involved," Turnipseed said.

Zeke nodded as he filled his mouth with another forkful of the delicious rice.

"Can you help us?" Famara asked.

"It's not our way to get involved in situations where we don't have full disclosure, but anything that will disrupt Prussian plans will get our support. I won't ask you for details. We all have our secrets."

Famara smiled. "Thank you."

"Dolph left immediately after your incident," Turnipseed said.

Famara smiled. "I suspected he would."

"He'll be on an airship for Prussia by morning'" Turnipseed said. "I can't get you out by airship because the terminals are being watched. We'll take you to Liverpool and you can sail to France."

"He'll have too much of a head start,' Famara argued. "I may lose him."

"You won't sail all the way," Turnipseed replied. "Once you get far enough out to sea we'll get you airborne."

Famara was puzzled. "How?"

Turnipseed smiled. "You'll see. Now eat and rest. We'll have to set out early for Liverpool."

Turnipseed regarded Zeke. "For the time being you are under the service of the Freedonian Dispatch. You are to stay with

Mr. Keita until his book his retrieved and returned."

Zeke shifted in his seat. "Sir...ah Reverend, I don't know if..."

"You'll be paid for your services."

Zeke smiled. "God bless Freedonia!"

Reverend Turnipseed smirked. "I'll see you in the morning."

21

Zeke and Famara awoke to the chilly surroundings of the East End church. Mrs. Morgan, George's mother, fixed a meal of porridge and fish to get them on their way followed by surprisingly good coffee. Reverend Turnipseed joined them when they were almost done. He took a bowl from Mrs. Morgan and began to eat.

"We have you listed as laborers," he said. You'll load a French freighter in London harbor then board with the last load," he said. George placed his empty bowl on the table. "One more thing; the Prussians are still in France. You'll have to be very careful."

Famara nodded, but Zeke looked confused.

"Still in France?" he said

"There was a war and France lost," Turnipseed said. "The whys and hows are not important. This entire continent suffers from the worst dysfunctional families ever. The result was that the Prussians won and demanded reparations from France. Their troops will remain until the payments are complete. If Dolph is on the continent he may have put the word out on you two, at least in Paris. We'll have to bypass our contact there and put you in contact with someone less conspicuous."

"And who would that be?' Famara asked.

Turnipseed grinned. "You'll find out when you get there."

Famara reached into his shirt and extracted his compass watch. The needle sat motionless, causing him to frown.

"The Prussian probably has a good head start on us."

Turnipseed waved his concerns away. "You'll catch up to him. Don't worry. Now if you gentlemen are done, you have a boat to catch."

George took them by wagon to London harbor. The anemic winter sun barely worked its light through the stubborn grey clouds. They followed George to the freighter then began their cover job, trying their best to look as if they knew what they were doing. Though Zeke struggled to look authentic, Famara fell in with the others as if born to the task. By the time they finished the last load and boarded with the crew the talented Malian had made a few friends.

They settled into a cramped cabin near the engine room then changed out of their clothes.

"You ain't no stranger to hard work," Zeke commented.

"My responsibility requires many skills," Famara replied. "It is not a glamorous life."

"So what did you do before you became a horro?" Zeke asked.

Famara looked at him puzzled. "I've always been a horro."

"What I meant was what did you do when you were younger?"

"I trained to become a horro," Famara replied.

Zeke shrugged. "So you don't know anything but being a horro."

Famara looked bewildered. "Of course not. Haven't you always been a bounty hunter?"

"Nope," Zeke replied. "I tried farming for a while. Just don't have the touch. I served in the Haitian army during the Reunion War then did a stint in New Haiti as a mercenary. I'm better with a gun than a plow. I got the knack of finding folks, too. But I gave it up once my daddy passed away. Momma needed help on the farm so I came home."

They were interrupted by a knock on the door. Zeke reached for his guns but Famara waved him away.

"We are among friends," he said.

Famara opened the door, revealing a dark brown man with a warm smile and heavy coat. He extended his hand.

"Gentlemen, I'm Percy Dawkins. If you'll follow me to the deck we'll get you fellows to France."

Zeke and Famara looked at each other in confusion.

"So you are the one who will get us airborne?" Famara asked.

"That I am," Percy replied. "Follow me, please."

Percy walked away. Famara and Zeke followed him to the deck with their belongings. When they emerged onto the deck a wide smile broke on Zeke's face. Famara looked with wonder.

"I'll be damned!" Zeke said.

"Fascinating!" Famara said.

A large flying craft rested on deck, swarmed by a team of men.

"That's one big Dragonfly," Zeke said.

"I think the proper terminology is cyclo-gyro," Famara said.

Percy smiled proudly. "You're both right. This is the latest evolution, Zeke. We call it a Grasshopper. It's designed to carry cargo and a few passengers. It's your ride to France."

Zeke trotted over to the boxes being loaded onto the Grasshopper. Famara circled the craft, his hands clasped behind his back, Percy at his side.

"I'm familiar with the function of the cyclo-gyro," he said.

"But to my knowledge no one had been able to build an actual flying craft."

"We've had gyros for almost ten years now," Percy said. "Dr. Carver and Thaddeus Banneker figured out how to make it work. Don't ask me how. I just fly them."

One of the prep team came up to them. "She's ready, sir."

Percy smiled at Famara. "Let's get airborne!"

When they reached the Grasshopper Zeke was already

seated, leather helmet and goggles on.

"What took y'all so long?" he said.

Percy looked at him suspiciously. "How'd you know how to put those things on? Flying is restricted to authorized personnel."

"I had a flyer friend who owed me a favor," Zeke said. "A bounty got too far ahead for me to ride him down so my friend gave me a lift."

Percy sucked his teeth then turned his attention to Famara. He helped the Malian get situated then climbed into the flyer's seat.

"Here we go!" Percy shouted. He waved his hand to the prep crew.

The prep crew started the Grasshopper's engine by spinning the horizontal propellers. The craft belched black smoke from the side exhaust as the propellers spun faster and faster. The Grasshopper lifted vertically, rising higher and higher over the freighter.

Zeke turned backwards to face Famara.

"You're going to love this!" he shouted over the thumping propellers.

Famara looked worried. "If you say so."

The Grasshopper tilted forward and they streaked ahead, disappearing into the mist and clouds.

The aircraft cruised across the churning English Channel to France. Zeke reveled in the journey, peering over the side to see the snow covered landscape streak by. Famara was distracted, his eyes fixed on his compass watch. Dolph had taken the book beyond the range of his device, which vexed him beyond what he revealed. For four years he'd searched for the missing tomes. Having the last one in his grasp then losing it almost caused him to lose his composure.

But anger wouldn't help him recover the book. He would trust the Freedonians for the time being. If this next contact did not produce positive results he would go on his own as before. He had little time to waste.

The Grasshopper flew north of Paris, sticking to the

countryside and avoiding any airships in the distance. Soon they soared above rolling mountains and deep verdant valleys, speckled by snow covered fields. The Grasshopper descended over one of the fields then circled. Zeke spotted a large castle perched on a steep hill overlooking the field. The gate opened and a group of riders emerged, riding swiftly down a winding road which terminated at the field. The Grasshopper stopped circling then made a vertical landing on the field. The riders waited until the propellers stilled before approaching the craft. They were led by a brown skinned woman draped in a luxurious sable coat, a top hat riding on her head. Riding pants and boots covered her shapely legs. Her beautiful face was twisted with annoyance.

The trio disembarked, the crisp air causing them to pull their coats tighter. The woman rode up to Percy, her face still cross.

"Mademoiselle Bijoux!" Percy exclaimed. "I have a delivery for you."

"Why are you here?" Mademoiselle Bijoux replied. "I wasn't notified."

"Paris was out of the question," he replied. "These two are being hunted by the Prussians."

"Then they are in more danger here."

She jumped from her horse then strode to Zeke, her hand extended.

"Annette Bijoux," she said.

Zeke took her hand and kissed it. "Zeke Culpepper at your service."

His gesture forced a smile to Annette's face. She went to Famara and introduced herself.

Famara did not take her hand. Instead he bowed slightly.

"Famara Keita," he said.

Annette bowed in returned then turned her attention back to Percy.

"I ask you again. Why are you here?"

"These men are seeking something and someone. We've

been instructed to help them."

Famara looked at his compass watch and smiled. "It's close. We're on the right track."

Annette walked up to Famara and gazed at the device.

"Interesting, however I wish you would have contacted me before you came. The situation here is not favorable."

"What are you talking about?" Percy asked.

"The Germans have decided to make Lorraine a part of their kingdom."

"How close are we to Lorraine?" Zeke asked.

"You're in it," Annette replied. "Normally I would offer you my hospitality but I'm more than certain a company of Prussians is making its way here as we speak. Your arrival was not necessarily discreet."

Annette went back to her horse and mounted. "We brought extra horses and coats."

"I'm not staying," Percy said. He looked at his two former passengers.

"You're in her hands now. Good luck."

Annette's men unloaded the Grasshopper then secured the supplies onto pack horses. Percy climbed back into the cyclo-gyro; in moments he was airborne and away.

Zeke and Famara mounted up.

"I have a villa in the mountains north of here," Annette said.

"My men will take you there. I'm going back to my home and wait for the Prussians."

"Maybe we should go with you," Famara said. "If we brought trouble we should help you deal with it."

"I can take care of myself," Annette replied. "Stay with my men and do as they say. I'll be along around nightfall."

Zeke, Famara, and the others rode across the field as Annette rode back to the castle.

Three hours later they reached the villa, a spacious stone

house hidden on a hillside overlooking a stream. Annette's men said nothing as they unpacked the duo's belongings then headed back to the castle. Famara and Zeke took inventory; there was ammunition, provisions and papers for identification. Zeke sat down then tinkered with his shotgun while Famara studied the maps included with their gear.

"We're close to the book," Famara said.

"Is that so?" Zeke asked without looking up.

"Yes. We should leave now. The compass watch will lead us to it."

"I think we should wait until Miss Bijoux comes," Zeke said.

"It wouldn't be polite to leave when she told us she was returning."

Famara frowned. "It's not necessary to wait."

Zeke looked up. "I know it's not. It's good manners."

Famara stared at Zeke for a moment then shrugged. A couple of hours passed, both men concentrating on their own matters. As the sun descended behind the hills the sound of hooves interrupted their silence. The door burst open and Annette's men entered. Two of the men were wounded, supported by two others.

One man was dragged in by his cohort. Annette followed with a Chassepot rifle in her gloved hands.

"The Prussians really want you," she said.

Zeke strapped on two ammo belts of shotgun shells. Famara grabbed a needle gun from the provisions and his throwing knives.

"How far are they behind you?" Famara asked.

"Not far," Annette answered.

"So I guess you need our services," Zeke said.

Annette grinned. "I guess I do."

"Is there a back way out?" Famara asked.

"Yes," Annette replied.

She led them to the rear door.

"You and your men stay inside. Come on, Zeke."

Zeke took his shotgun out of his leg holster then slung a rifle across his back. Together they exited the rear door.

"You thinking about setting up a crossfire?" Zeke asked.

Famara nodded. "The two of us should be able to put up enough firepower to drive them off."

Zeke loaded the shotgun. "That might not be enough."

"Let's hope it is."

They split up, Zeke heading right, Famara left. They slipped into the dense forest then worked their way along the road until they were about ten yards distant. Famara settled in behind a thick tree, familiarizing himself with his rifle. Zeke kissed his cross then tucked it into his shirt. He worked his way close to the road, his shotgun at the ready. Ten minutes later the sound of horses could be heard. The Prussian riders came into view draped in elaborate uniforms and plumed hats, their sabers drawn. Famara and Zeke waited until they were all in view before firing. Five Prussians went down with the first volley; three more were felled by a volley from the villa. The others quickly dismounted and ran for the cover of the woods. The first man to the right was blown back onto the road by Zeke's shotgun. Those to the left were struck by Famara's throwing knives. The shadows held no respite for the Prussians; they fled to the mounts under fire. Three managed to mount and ride away.

Famara walked into the road. Zeke ran to the nearest horse, climbed on then rode away.

"Zeke! No!" Famara shouted.

Zeke chased the Prussians. The horse he chose was swift, catching up to its cohorts in minutes. Zeke raised his shotgun and fired, blowing the closest Prussian off his mount. He fired again, killing the second rider. The last Prussian turned his horse about, pulled his saber then charged. Zeke pulled his trigger; his shotgun was empty. He ducked the swing meant to decapitate him then twisted in his saddle to avoid a thrust at his ribs. He blocked another swipe with his gun, but it was obvious his luck was running slim. The Prussian suddenly pulled up, then fell from his mount. A throwing knife protruded from the back of his neck.

Zeke turned to see Famara ride up to him.

"That was stupid," Famara said.

"It was necessary," Zeke replied. "If these fellas got back they'd bring more friends. If they don't show up we'll maybe have a little more time to get where we're going."

Famara nodded. "Let's get back to the villa."

When they returned to the villa Annette and the others were tending their wounded. Annette wiped her hands.

"What happened?"

"They're dead," Zeke said. "We need to be moving. More will come. Y'all probably need to come with us."

"That won't be necessary," Annette said. "If anyone else comes my men will tell them you attacked the villa and took me hostage."

Famara looked confused. "Took you hostage?"

Annette smiled. "Your device might tell you some things, but I know this country. I'll take you as far as I can."

Famara looked at Zeke and Zeke shrugged. "She's got a point."

"Come then, we must be on our way," Famara said.

The three of them gathered provisions then mounted their steeds. They headed north, into the snow-capped peaks.

22

Menna arrived in Tripoli in the cover of darkness. She was exhausted from the hard journey, yet a smile graced her face under her shesh. She halted her camel just outside the city then set up her tent. She'd wait until morning before entering, for she would need directions to find the Prussian embassy. She would also need time to prepare. There would be no exposed knives this time, no coercion for secrets. She would have to be more diplomatic, which meant she would use other skills to obtain what she wanted. She disrobed, shedding the clothing of a warrior for the traditional garb of an Ihaggaren woman. The last item she removed was her shesh, revealing her lovely countenance marred by a frown. Men thought her attractive which would serve her well when she decided to marry.

Her appearance also served its purpose when seeking information, but it was a tactic she rarely used. Her skill with knives was more efficient and left fewer consequences. She slept, awaking at the first light. After a quick meal of bread and tea she took out her mirror then decorated her face as was the tradition, scowling as she did so. By mid morning her disguise was complete. She packed her belongings, mounted her camel then rode into Tripoli.

Though donning the clothes was easy, assuming the attitude was more difficult. Ihaggaren women were known to be strong willed and independent, but it would serve her purpose better to be less so among the Arabs. She ignored their leers and comments, working her way through the city until she spotted the building flying the Prussian flag. She guided the camel to the entrance then dismounted. The guards studied her emotionlessly as she approached.

"What is your business here?" one of the guards asked in flawless Arabic.

"I am here on behalf of El Tellak," she said. "I wish to speak to the ambassador."

The guard's expression turned sour at the mention of her brother's name.

"Wait here," he said.

The guard went into the embassy, leaving Menna with his companion. She ignored his stares and smile as she waited. The other guard returned, waving her inside.

"Follow me," he said.

She followed the guard into the building. The office was smaller than she expected; the ambassador sat at large ebony wood desk bent over a sheet of paper. His left hand held the paper in place as he scribbled across it with his right.

"Leave us," he said without looking up.

The guard clicked his heels then bowed sharply before walking away.

The man waited until the guard closed the door behind her before setting his pen down then looking up. His lean, angular face was bordered by a thin beard. His expression was not pleasant.

"Why are you here?" he asked.

"I was sent by El Tellak to ask for your assistance in an important matter," she said.

The ambassador leaned back in his seat then entwined his fingers, a hint of a smile coming to his face.

"And what does El Tellak want?"

"He wishes to know the whereabouts of a Soninke man named Famara Keita."

"And why does El Tellak think we would share such

information with him?"

Menna's patience was slowly draining away. "He is the man who disrupted the exchange for the book. We wish to exact revenge."

"Really?" The ambassador stood then took a cigarette from the silver case embossed with his initials resting on his desk.

"El Tellak failed us. We gave him an assignment and he botched it. We owe him nothing."

"Then I will bother you no more," Menna said. She turned to leave.

"Wait one minute," the ambassador said. "That's it? You're leaving?"

Menna turned to face the man. "You have refused to share information with me. I will find other means."

The ambassador took a long drag on his cigarette then slowly exhaled.

"I thought you would try to be more persuasive," he said as he grinned.

Menna smiled then sauntered toward the ambassador, stopping when their noses almost touched.

"You mean like this?"

She slammed her left hand into his throat then pushed him back onto his desktop. In a flash she yanked the dagger from her dress then pressed it against his cheek.

"Now you will tell me what I want to know or..."

"Gott im Himmel!"

Menna let go of the ambassador then spun away before the guard was able to bring his rifle to his shoulder. She threw her dagger into his throat then sprinted to him as he fell, snatching the knife free. She met the other guard as he tried to rush through the door, grabbing his rifle then pulling him inside. She cut his throat as she snatched the rifle from his hand. She spun about to see the ambassador rummaging through his desk drawer with his right hand while holding his bruised neck with his left; by the time he found his revolver Menna aimed the rifle at his head.

"Put it down," she said.

The ambassador placed the handgun back into his desk drawer then raised his hands.

"Please! I don't know..."

Menna shot him in the shoulder. He twirled like a crippled ballerina then fell to the floor. She threw the rifle to the floor then walked around the desk to the wounded ambassador.

"Where is Famara Keita?" she asked.

"I...our reports say he is in England."

Menna grinned. "Thank you."

"You won't get away with this," the ambassador croaked. "The authorities will be notified!"

"No they won't." Menna cut the ambassador's throat.

She hurried from the embassy, mounted her camel then rode away. Her plans had gone awry, but she gained the information she needed. She would go to Egypt then catch an airship to England. Once she arrived she would find Famara Keita then kill him. It would be that simple.

23

Annette led Zeke and Famara to the road north, the highway that would eventually take them to Prussia. After an hour Famara reined his horse to a standstill.

"What's wrong?" Zeke asked.

"We're going the wrong way."

Annette joined them moments later.

"Gentlemen, I hate to interrupt your conversation but we have to keep moving. There is a tavern with a small lodge that we'll make just before dark if we hurry."

Famara looked up from his compass watch. "We're going the wrong way."

"This is the way to Prussia," Annette replied.

"It may be, but it is not the way to the book. The compass says we must head south."

"Your compass is wrong," Annette said.

Famara's look was not pleasant. "The compass is never wrong."

Annette made a face just as arrogant as Famara's. "That's impossible. Bavaria is to the south. The Bavarians and the Prussians are not the best of friends."

Zeke took off his hat then scratched his head. "Wait a minute. I thought this was all one place."

Annette shook her head. "The German kingdoms act as one but they are not officially a nation. Prussia dominates but the other kingdoms still hold on to some independence, especially those in the south."

"That was informative, but it still doesn't change the fact that my compass tells us to go south," Famara said.

Zeke replaced his hat. "Ma'am, I don't know you or this place that well but what I do know is that that compass has been right every time. If I was a betting man I'd bet on it."

"This makes no sense," Annette said. "Lead the way then!"

They traveled south, following winding roads that climbed the rising heights then meandered along the Rhine River. It was almost dark when the shadow of an imposing castle looming over the nearby river stole their light.

"There," Famara said. "The book is inside the castle."

Annette opened her mouth as if to speak but then closed it.

"Well, if it's in that castle the Prussians are close as well," Zeke said.

Famara nodded in agreement. "We need a place to stay."

"Follow me," Annette finally said.

She led them to a small village nestled into a crook in the river. The streets were empty save for the horses tethered before a small tavern. The smell of sausage and beer drifted in the air. Zeke rubbed his stomach then licked his lips.

"Didn't realize how hungry I was until right now."

Annette smiled. "There's plenty of food inside."

"Wait a minute," Zeke said. "Won't we...stand out?"

"Don't worry about that," Annette replied. "This is not America or even Freedonia for that matter."

They hitched their horses and entered the tavern. Long tables stretched across the room, occupied by a scattered crowd of folks who looked up at the trio when they entered. A woman ambled from the kitchen, wiping her hands on her apron as she approached. She looked at the three of them before her eyes settled on Annette.

"Kann ich Ihnen helfin?"

Annette nodded. "Wir brauchen einen ort zum verveilen."

"Annette?" The gruff male voice came from the far end of one of the tables. A thick red faced man stuffed in a dusty suit hurried toward them.

"Annette Bijoux?"

Annette bowed. "The one and only."

The man grinned. "I can't believe it. Annette Bijoux is here in our village!"

The man grabbed Annette's wrist then pulled her to the front of the tavern.

"Everyone, your attention please! The amazing Annette Bijoux is in our humble village!"

The onlookers clapped with star struck admiration. Zeke pushed back his hat then scratched his hairline.

"What in God's name is going on?" he said.

"I have no idea," Famara replied.

"You've obviously travelled a long way to get here," the man said. "You are hungry, no?"

"Famished," Annette replied.

"Hilda! Bring our guest food!" the man shouted. He led the three to a nearby table. Chairs were brought for them and plates filled with food set before them.

The man sat beside them. "I am Helmut Baum. You can't believe how excited I am to see you. This is truly an honor!"

Annette blushed. "Thank you, Helmut."

"I saw your last performance in Paris ten years ago. All of France was there."

Annette giggled. "Not all of France. I'm sure there were a few sailors that didn't make it."

Helmut Baum let loose a boisterous laugh. "Indeed, indeed."

He stood. "You must grace us with a song!"

Annette looked away. "It's been a long time since I sang for an audience."

"I own this tavern and the lodge next door. Sing a song and you and your friends can spend the night for free."

Annette stood. "It would be hard for me to sing without music."

Helmut scurried to the back then returned with a guitar.

"I can't play, unfortunately," he said.

"Neither can I," Annette admitted.

"I can." Zeke finished off a sausage then stood.

"All I know is Mississippi music," he said.

Annette beamed. "Perfect! You know Kinfolk Corner Blues?"

Zeke laughed. "Who doesn't?"

Zeke took a few moments to tune the old instrument then fell into a slow work song rhythm. Annette closed her eyes, patting her hand against her hip in time with Zeke's tapping foot. Then she let loose a moan that shook Zeke and Famara to the core. This petite genteel woman had the voice of a bayou angel. The entire tavern swayed with Zeke's cadence. Even Famara dropped his serious countenance, rocking his head from side to side to the rhythm.

'Came home from church one Sunday,
My man done up and gone.
Came home from church one Sunday,
My man done up and gone.
Now I'm standing on Kinfolk Corner,
Wonderin' where that man done run.

Looked for that man on Monday,
Tuesday did the same
Said I looked for that man on Monday,
Tuesday did the same,
Met a fine young man on Wednesday
Put my long lost man to shame.

That fine man put his arms around me,
Told me things going be alright
I said that fine man here he hugged me,
Said things going be alright,
He said he'll love me in the morning,
And he'd rock me through the night.

Came home from church one Sunday
My old man done run away.
Came home from church one Sunday,
My old man done run away.
Now I'm smiling on Kinfolk Corner,
'Cause my new man's gonna stay!

Annette finished with a crescendo of emotions, drawing enthusiastic applause from the tavern folk.

"Excellent! Magnificent!"

The voice uttering those words was familiar to Zeke. He looked up at Famara, his eyes narrowed.

"It's Dolph," he whispered. "And he's got friends."

Zeke eased the guitar to the floor then slowly reached into his jacket and gripped his revolver. He looked up at Famara and the horro nodded back at him, his hand inside his robe. Zeke assumed he held a revolver as well, but his short time with his reluctant companion taught him to expect the unexpected.

"Wait," Annette said.

Zeke peeked around Famara. Five burly men left their meals then gathered before Dolph and his companions. Zeke looked at Helmut. The tavern owner's jovial expression was gone, replaced by a scowl.

"Excuse me. I have business to attend to."

He went into the kitchen then returned with a shotgun.

"Herr Baum!" Dolph called out. "'Is this how you treat you guests?"

Baum sauntered to the door. The men stepped aside.

"What are you doing here, Prussian?" Helmut said.

"I prefer Oberst Errickson."

"Take you men and leave," Helmut said. "You know the agreement. You get the castle and nothing more."

Dolph flashed a predatory grin. "We had no intentions of gracing your hovel until we heard that lovely voice. Such a beautiful sound coming from such a lowly Negress."

Zeke started pulling his revolver from his shirt.

"Don't," Annette whispered. "I've been called worse. Let Helmut handle this."

Helmut raised his shotgun. "I will not allow you to insult my guest. Now back to your castle, Prussian."

Dolph's face hardened. "When we are a formal nation, the Prussians will stand above all others. You will regret your behavior."

Helut's expression remained unchanged. "Maybe then, but not now. Get out of my tavern."

Dolph and his men backed out of the tavern. Helmut slapped the men on the back.

"Thank you, boys. Beer is on the house."

He strolled back to the trio, the shotgun tucked under his arm.

"I apologize, Mademoiselle Bijoux. The Prussians can be inconvenient."

"No need to apologize. You handled the situation well."

"I had to. If not your friends were prepared to do worse."

Helmut smiled at Zeke and Famara.

"Now tell me, what have the Prussians done to you?"

"They have something very valuable to me," Famara said. "I've come to take it back."

"If they have it, it's in the castle," Helmut said.

"Why are the Prussians in Bavaria?" Annette asked.

"I don't know," Helmut replied. "A gentleman came to me

two years ago inquiring about the castle. He wished to use it as a toy factory so I sold it to him. I've been trying to get rid of the thing for years. He told me he would require complete privacy. In return he and his workers would never come into town. We signed an agreement and three days later the airships began to arrive, delivering men and supplies. They never use wagons, only airships. And they kept their agreement until Oberst Eriksson arrived a few months ago."

"How do we get into the castle?" Famara asked.

"That will be difficult. The roads leading to the castle are guarded by towers and men in some type of metal suits. They look like Teutonic Knights but they move like dancers. And of course the towers are manned."

"There must be a way in," Zeke said. "Nobody is gonna wrap themselves tight like that without a way out."

"They have the airships," Annette said.

"I'm not talking about now," Zeke said. "That castle is old. Whoever holed up in it a long time ago had to have a way out once things got heated."

Helmut smiled. "You're right...Zeke."

"A tunnel?" Famara asked.

Helmut nodded.

"Take us there."

"Not tonight. I wouldn't be able to find it in the dark. You can eat, rest, and maybe Mademoiselle Bijoux and Zeke will grace us with another song. In the morning I'll take you to the tunnel."

24

Zeke and Famara were up and ready at first light. Annette met them in the dining hall just as eager. Helmut strolled in from the kitchen with plates of weisswurst with sweet mustard and pretzels.

"It's a long journey. You must eat first."

After the delicious meal they set out. They rode the winding trails for half the day before stopping near a dense growth of trees surrounding an inlet from the river.

"The old master used to keep a boat here for a hasty escape,"

Helmut said. He led them into the thicket until they came to a wall of rock. Helmut pushed vines and shrubs aside to reveal the tunnel entrance.

"I've never been inside, but I heard it leads to the castle basement."

"Thank you Helmut," Famara said. They shook hands.

"I hope I will see you again," he said.

"I hope so, too," Zeke answered.

Annette took her rifle from her horse. Zeke and Famara loaded their packs on their backs. Zeke checked his shotgun and Famara studied his compass. Together they entered the darkness of the tunnel.

Daylight soon failed them, the way ahead not completely dark but difficult to see as they went deeper into the tunnel

"Wait," Famara said.

He took off his pack then sat it on the damp stone. He rustled about inside then extracted a foot long brass tube and at small crank. He attached the crank to the end of the tube then turned it rapidly. As he turned light appeared at the other end of the tube. After a few more minutes the light was intense enough to illuminate the tunnel.

"I'll be damned...I mean Lord have mercy," Zeke said.

Annette touched the tube, her face curious.

"Fascinating," she said.

"The turning of the crank generates electricity which activates the light," Famara explained. "Come, we must hurry."

Famara and Annette proceeded down the tunnel. Zeke took off his pack, holstered his shotgun then leaned against the wall. He took his cross out of his shirt and rubbed it with his hand. The other two were barely visible when they realized Zeke wasn't following. When they returned Famara was not happy.

"What are you doing?" he asked.

"I'm thinking," Zeke replied.

"This is not the best time for you to become contemplative."

"I've been chasing this book halfway around the world," Zeke said. "First for Pierre, now for you."

"You're being paid well," Famara said.

Annette stepped between them. "Gentlemen, once again you choose an inopportune time for discussion. I suggest..."

Zeke's cold glare cut Annette off. Her hands tightened about her rifle.

"Excuse me ma'am, but my friend and I are talking," Zeke said.

"I have a question, and the answer to that question will determine whether I take another step down this tunnel or turn around and catch the next airship home."

"What is it, Zeke?" Famara asked.

"I got a feeling that once we get inside that castle a whole lot folks are going to end up dead. Maybe even us. So before I go blasting more folks to Glory, I need to know what I'm doing it for. I need to know what's in that book of yours that makes it so important."

The look on Annette's face reflected his decision. Famara sighed, took off his pack then sat.

"There is a city in my homeland that is ancient, older than anything, even the Great Pyramids. It's been known by many names over the centuries; Dierra, Agada, Gana and Silla. It rose to great heights and fell just as deep again and again. But with every resurrection it loomed greater than its previous incarnation. That city is Wagadu. The Elders are the stewards of Wagadu, and I am but one of its guardians."

Zeke pushed back his hat. "That's all well and good, but what does that have do to with the book?

"Be quiet and listen," Annette scolded. "You have no sense of history."

She nodded to Famara. "Please continue mon frère."

"Wagadu contains the secrets of time, wonders we have yet to rediscover. When it was known as Gana its greatest king decreed that the secrets be recorded in books to preserve the knowledge of the ancestors. The jeles, oral history keepers, protested but the king would not be denied. When Gana fell to the Almoravids, the books were entrusted to the kingdom of Mali. From Mali they were passed to Songhai where some of the tomes found a sacred home in Timbuktu. It was there where our scholars discovered the secret of the books."

Famara fell silent.

"Well?" Zeke urged.

"The scholars discovered that while some of the books contained script, others were filled with patterns and shapes that made no sense. One of the elders who studied under George Washington Carver saw something familiar in the patterns. He took the wires of a telegraph then attached them to the patterns with the telegraph on the opposite end. The electricity flowed through the patterns to the telegraph faster than any wire could conduct it."

"So what are you telling us?" Zeke asked.

"If the pages were duplicated then miniaturized, the patterns could disperse energy at an amazing speed, making electric powered machines much more efficient. But there is one problem. We cannot identify the material from which the patterns were drawn."

"So what does this have to do with the Prussians?" Annette asked.

Famara's face became hard.

"It seems that money can loosen the most dedicated tongues. Not long after our discovery Timbuktu was raided by Tuaregs. They obtained the books then fled into the desert. I was sent after them. It took me two years as a Tuareg slave, an eklan, to discover where they were hidden. The Tuaregs shared what they knew about the books freely with anyone interested in buying them. The Prussians were the only people to respond. Them and an American antique collector."

Zeke nodded. "'So that's how Pierre got the book."

"Not exactly. The men who sold the book to Pierre stole it from the antique dealer. I was able to thwart the Prussians in Mali. Once I returned the other books I was sent for this one."

Zeke still wasn't satisfied. "So what do the Prussians want with the books?"

"They'll use the pages to operate their weapons," Annette answered.

"Exactly," Famara said. "The knowledge of the books was meant for much more."

Famara stood. "That is all I'll reveal to you. Either come with us or leave."

Zeke tucked his cross back into his shirt then took out his shotgun.

"Lead the way."

They followed the tunnel until it narrowed to an opening the size of a normal door. The hinges were on their side but there was no handle. The sound of machinery buzzed on the opposite side. Zeke stepped forward, extracting his knife. He prodded about until he found a soft spot. He pushed the knife in then worked open the door.

"Here we go," he whispered.

Famara shut off the light as Zeke eased open the portal, revealing a dimly lit room filled with a cluster of machines. There seemed to be no one about despite the activity.

"We need to get a closer look," Famara said. "Annette, stay here and cover us."

"How will I do that?" Annette said. "I can't see a thing."

Famara reached into his bag and extracted a pair or green tinted goggles.

"Put these on."

Annette donned the glasses.

"Amazing! I can see like it's daylight!"

"So why didn't we use those in the tunnel?" Zeke asked.

"It's my only pair," Famara answered. "I didn't plan on companions."

Famara turned to Annette. "Zeke and I will take a look. I suspect Dolph is overseeing the manufacture of weapons that will utilize the pages of the book. If he is, we'll get the book then blow this place up."

Zeke looked confused. "Blow it up with what?"

Famara went into his pack again. He took out a uniquely curved knife with a long handle. He unscrewed the handle, stuck two fingers inside and extracted a stick of dynamite.

"I have more than enough," Famara said with a smile.

"Lord have mercy," Zeke said. "Ain't you full of surprises."

"Are you with me?" Famara asked.

Zeke cocked his shotgun.

"Let's do this," he said.

Zeke and Famara stayed low as they crept down the incline to the factory floor. Assembly stations lined the stone walkway, each station cluttered with a collection of brass arms, legs and torsos.

"Looks like this is where they built that armored man we ran into in London," Zeke whispered.

Famara approached one of the stations. "No, these are smaller. This looks like personal armor."

Zeke pushed back his hat. "I don't know of any armor these days that will stop a bullet."

"It's possible with the right knowledge, the kind of knowledge the book can provide if used properly," Famara replied.

"Something tells me you're not telling me everything about that book."

Famara smiled at Zeke.

"You know what you need to know for now."

"Remind me never to play poker with you," Zeke commented.

Famara picked up a large square panel from the cluttered work bench, turning it about in his hand.

"The Prussians have figured out how the pages work," he said. "But they still don't know everything."

He turned to Zeke. "The book is here, probably close by. They'll use the pages to activate these suits."

"Activate?" Zeke took his hat off then scratch his head.

"What exactly are you talking about?"

"He's talking about the power of electricity."

Bright light flooded the factory room. Zeke and Famara crouched lower as ten armored men strolled out onto a raised platform. The last man to enter was Dolph. He wore the armor as well but he carried the helmet under his arm. A smug smile graced his handsome Nordic face.

"Do you like my castle, Famara Keita?" he asked. "Yes, I know your name and I know who you work for. The Tuaregs are a bit unruly but they are very good at gathering information at the right price."

Famara didn't respond. Instead he reached into his jacket and took out a throwing knife.

"I haven't discovered who your Freedonian friend is, but it doesn't matter," Dolph continued. "Neither of you will leave this room, at least not alive."

The fact that he said 'neither' meant he wasn't aware of Annette.

"Why are you doing this?" Famara asked. "What purpose does it serve?"

"The purpose of power," Dolph replied. "But I don't expect you Africans to understand that. You waste your time fighting each other for your paltry spoils instead of realizing there is a world ripe for plunder. Your elders sit on the power of the ages and do nothing with it. Even my superiors fail to realize the potential of the pages of your so-called book."

"That man seems full of himself," Zeke whispered. "I should shoot him in the throat."

"Let him talk," Famara answered. "It gives me more time."

"Time for what?"

Famara smiled.

"The Age of Steam is over," Dolph said. "The future belongs to electricity and your book will unleash its power!"

Zeke was tired of Dolph's bravado and apparently he was not alone. A shot rang out, the bullet striking the armored man closest to Dolph.

"That's my girl!" Zeke said.

Dolph ducked for cover as the soldiers turned in Annette's direction. Before they could fire Zeke sprang up, his shotgun raised. He unloaded his gun at the soldiers, the lead buckshot peppering the metal. Famara grabbed two throwing knives then smacked the ends against the floor. There was a pop then the handles ignited. The horro stood then threw the knives at the platform.

"Down!' he yelled.

The knives exploded as soon as they struck the platform, filling the factory with sound and smoke.

"Let's go!" Zeke shouted.

"No, we have to destroy all of this!" Famara said

"With what?"

Famara took out more knives. "These."

Zeke grinned. "I'll cover you."

They sprinted through the factory, throwing knives and blowing up everything in sight. A few armor soldiers went up as well, struck by Famara's knives. Zeke took down more, the armor unable to stop a point blank shotgun blast. Annette continued to fire from her hiding place, adding to the confusion.

Once Famara was satisfied they worked their way back to Annette.

"Nice shooting, ma'am," Zeke said.

"Merci."

"Can we go now?" Zeke said to Famara.

"No. We came for the book."

"I believe your book is somewhere down here burning."

"Dolph is many things but he's not a fool," Famara said.

"The book is upstairs in the castle. We're going to get it."

Zeke looked at Annette and she nodded. He shrugged then loaded more shells in his shotgun.

"Lead the way," he said.

The horro stood, and then the chatter of an automatic gun filled the room. Zeke jerked Famara back down. He was too late. Famara fell onto him bleeding from several places. The horro looked at his wounds in bewilderment.

"By the ancestors," he whispered.

"Jesus Christ!" Zeke exclaimed. He and Annette tore pieces from Famara's shirt to stop the bleeding.

"Don't worry about me," Famara said. "You have to stop Dolph."

"I'm not worried about that German right now, I'm worried about..."

Famara grabbed Zeke's collar then yanked him so close their noses almost touched.

"You have to stop him!" Famara shouted. "What he possesses is too valuable to lose."

"Is it worth your life?" Zeke asked.

"Yes," Famara answered without hesitation.

The two men stared at each other for a long moment before Zeke spoke.

"Give me your revolver and your rifle."

Famara handed over the weapons.

"And your trick knives."

Famara took the knives from his jacket and handed them to Zeke. Zeke shoved them into his waist belt.

"Dolph is most likely heading for the roof," Famara said. He winced before continuing. "My guess is there's an airship waiting."

Zeke secured the weapons then began unloading his shotgun. He replaced the original shells with another set in brass casings.

"What are those?" Annette asked.

Zeke smiled. "I call 'em Mule Kickers. I didn't want to use them at first. Wasn't sure this government gun could handle 'em. I guess I'm about to find out."

Annette grabbed his arm. "Wait Zeke. You can't do this alone. There will be another chance to get the book."

"Pardon my language ma'am, but I'm damn sick and tired of that book. God didn't bless me with many talents, but the one He did give me will get me to the top of that roof. What happens then I don't know."

"I'll pray for you," she said.

"Pray for the Prussians," Zeke answered.

He hit the hilt of a throwing knife on the floor, sparking the fuse. Zeke threw the knife in the direction of the rapid fire gun and waited. No sooner did the knife explode did he jump from cover then sprint into the smoke. He emerged before two armored men. The third lay on his back struggling to rise. Zeke fired, the shotgun barking almost as loud as the knife bomb. The armored men flew off their feet in opposite directions with gaping holes in their torsos; he shot the third man and he fell still.

Zeke jammed the shotgun back into his leg holster then took out his revolvers. He wanted to save his shells just in case he ran into more armored men. What he did run into was a group of Prussian soldiers at the base of a spiral staircase. They turned simultaneously.

"Stop him!" one of them cried.

Zeke emptied his revolvers into the Prussians before they could lift a rifle. He jumped over the bodies then bolted up the stairs. As he neared the roof he heard the familiar sound of airship propellers. He hesitated before opening the roof door, and then kicked it open. Cold wind struck his face and he blinked; when he opened his eyes he saw Dolph running for the waiting airship, a satchel gripped in his right hand. Zeke raised his revolvers then pulled the triggers just as he remembered he'd emptied them. He dropped the guns, snatched out the shotgun and fired. The slug from the Mule Kicker shell smacked Dolph square in the back, the impact lifting him off his feet then pushing him and the satchel into the air, then over the roof edge.

Zeke ran to the edge of the roof with his shotgun at the ready, expecting fire from the airship. Instead the craft rose slowly then drifted away. Zeke thought about taking a parting shot, but holstered the gun. There had been enough killing this day.

He strolled to the roof edge. Below him was a tangle of dense woods. Neither Dolph nor the satchel was anywhere to be seen.

"Now this just ain't right," Zeke said. "Ain't right at all."

He turned then ambled back to the staircase.

25

Dolph opened his eyes to snow tinged treetops and gray skies. His breath frosted before his face as he tried to move then winched. The castle towers from which he fell slowly materialized before him as the pain in his back increased. He reached behind with his right hand, touching the spot where the pain emanated expecting the worse. He raised his fingers then smiled. There was no blood, but he knew something was broken.

He tried to sit up but the pain forced him back down. He was thankful his rear armor held, and he was also thankful the combination of tree limbs and his chute which cushioned his fall. He wanted to lie still for a few moments longer but he dared not. The African and the Freedonian might not be thorough, but he knew that damned Bavarian burgermeister would be. A patrol would scour the woods for his remains and he was determined to disappoint them.

He turned over and discovered the book. It survived the fall protected in the padded satchel. Another form of the padding had saved Dolph's life. He always wore it as extra precaution, another miracle from the African books. He picked up the satchel as he sat up then used a nearby sapling to stand. His legs were uninjured. He walked as fast as he could, his destination a secluded cove on the nearby river. He reached the cove then uncovered the boat he'd hidden for just such a situation. Clinching his teeth against the pain he placed the satchel into the boat then climbed in. He shoved the boat away from the shore then paddled the best he could into the slow river current. Luckily for him winter had yet to descend on Bavaria in full fury, therefore the river had not frozen. Dolph paddled until the current embraced the boat. He pulled the oars in then lay on his back, letting the flow to take him to his next destination.

The Switzerland site had been a last minute decision. He was sure he could convince the Reichstag of the importance of his mission but he was skeptical of how long it would hold their interest. The debacle in North Africa severely shortened his timetable, but he was prepared. The incident in Bavaria unnerved him. This horro was much cleverer than he expected, especially for an African. The Freedonian was no surprise; he was a man who shot before he thought, so he would be easy to deal with if encountered again. Still, Dolph had to admire his skill with his weapons.

He dosed off a number of times as his boat drifted down the river, awakened when the current had run it aground. This time he opened his eyes to grand mountains on either side of the river. He was in Switzerland. He could no longer afford sleep, for he would have to be vigilant to spot his mooring. Grabbing his paddle he pushed back into the river then did the best he could maneuvering the boat in the increasingly fast current. He remembered the task being much easier when he first mapped out the escape route, but at the time he didn't have broken bones. After struggling down the river for at least an half an hour the mooring appeared, a sliver of wood protruding from a stand of dense poplar trees along the rocky bank. He worked the boat through the rocks, finally reaching the mooring. He smiled when he saw the rope; the Swiss kept their bargain, maintaining the mooring in pristine condition despite it never being used. He struggled from the boat onto the pier then secured the craft before removing the satchel. Once on the dock he reached into his jacket then extracted a small communicator similar to the one he used for contacting Georg and Tomas. He cursed as he remembered the two, both dead at the hands of the African and the

Freedonian. The casualties of war, but it still didn't make him fell any less angry. He cranked the communicator for a full two minutes then sat on the pier. Fatigue crept up on him and he dozed again, only waking when the shrill call of a steam whistle penetrated his slumber. He sat up then gathered his things as the stream car pulled up to the pier. Sitting in the driver seat was Hansel Clements, the overseer for his secondary laboratory. The young man frowned as Dolph limped to the steam car then climbed in.

"You're early," Hansel said.

"That can't be helped," Dolph replied. "Our Bavarian laboratory was compromised."

Fear pervaded the young Swiss chemist's face. "Prussians?"

Dolph shook his head. "No. It seems the Africans are not happy we claimed their books. They sent someone to retrieve them, and he is better than I would have imagined."

Hansel seemed to relax. "You are here now. I always thought the Bavarian facility was too out in the open. We will have no such problems here."

"Still, I think we should release the cats just in case," Dolph said. "I wouldn't underestimate this man. I have done so to out detriment."

Hansel shrugged. "I see you have another book."

Dolph smiled. "Yes. The African is good, but not that good."

Both men laughed.

"Let's be on our way," Dolph said. "It's time we found out what secrets this book holds."

"Yes indeed!" Hansel answered.

Hansel climbed back into the driver's seat. They sped off into the Alps, a triumphant look on Dolph's face.

26

Zeke reached the main floor of the castle when the doors broke open. A group of Bavarian militiamen tumbled inside, followed by Helmut Braun in an ill-fitting officer's uniform. The men scrambled into formation then raised their rifles at Zeke. The Freedonian grinned as he raised his hands in surrender.

"Lower your rifles!" Helmut yelled.

The militiamen responded reluctantly, staring at Zeke with suspicious eyes.

"I'm so sorry, Zeke," Helmut said. "We heard the explosions and came as soon as we could."

Helmut looked about at Zeke's grim work. "It seems we weren't needed. Where is Dolph?"

"Outide," Zeke replied.

"We'll search for him immediately!" Helmut shouted.

He turned to his men. "Suchen Sie in den Wäldern für die preußische!"

Half of the militiamen hurried from the castle.

"Where is Fraulein Bijoux?"

"She's with Famara," Zeke answered. "Follow me."

Zeke led Helmut and his soldiers into the burning basement factory. Helmut eyes widened when he Annette next to Famara with blood stains on her clothes.

"Fraulein Bijoux! Are you alright?"

"I'm fine Herr Braun," Annette replied. "My friend is not so good."

Helmut gestured to them both. "Nehmen Sie ihn sofort ins Krankenhaus!"

The remaining militiamen gathered around Famara then gently lifted him, carrying him to the castle entrance.

"Where is the book?" Famara said as they carried him away.

"In the woods with Dolph," Zeke replied.

Famara looked suspicious. "You must retrieve it!"

Zeke smirked. "Ain't no need to be in a hurry. Dolph ain't going anywhere, 'cept to hell."

"Go with them," Famara urged. "Make sure you get the book."

Zeke followed the militiamen outside and into the woods. He looked up at the castle, trying to gauge where Dolph and the satchel would have landed. To his surprise there was nothing there. He searched the area in more detail, making wider circles but coming up with nothing. He squatted by a nearby tree, pushing back his hat as he studied the area more closely.

"Well, I'll be damned," he said.

He picked up the trail a good distance from where he suspected Dolph hit the ground. How he survived the fall Zeke couldn't figure out. The signs led to a cove that connected to a nearby river.

"That Prussian thought of everything," Zeke said out loud. "Famara ain't gonna be too happy about this."

Zeke headed back. By the time he reached the castle the others had evacuated to the village. The fire had spread into the upper region of structure, flames licking from the windows and black smoke curling into the clouds. A militiaman gestured for Zeke to follow him to the village.

Famara lay in bed attended by a trio of Bavarian nurses. Annette sat by his side holding his hand. Helmut stood close by, staring dreamily at Annette. Famara sat up.

"Where's the book?" he asked.

"With Dolph, I suspect," Zeke said.

Famara tried to sit up but one of the nurses eased him back down.

"Where is Dolph?" he asked.

Zeke pushed his hat back. "Now I can't answer that. Seems like your friend has nine lives. If you told me yesterday that a man could survive a fall that far with a slug in his back I would have said you were crazy."

"He's alive?" Annette said.

Zeke nodded.

Famara pounded his fist on his bed.

"Zeke, bring me my compass!" he said.

Zeke went to the dresser and retrieved Famara's contraption.

The horro gazed at the device then managed a smile.

"Good, it's still tracking, but I don't know how long" he said. He looked at Zeke and Annette with intense eyes.

"You must go after him," he said.

"That's going to be kind of hard," Zeke replied. "I know that trinket of yours can hunt down that book like a bloodhound, but I don't know heads or tails of this place."

"I do," Annette answered.

Zeke and Famara shared surprised looks.

"I can't ask you do to this," Famara said.

"No we can't," Zeke added. "You've been exposed to enough danger, ma'am."

"Apparently you haven't paid attention, Mr. Culpepper," Annette replied. "I can take care of myself. And besides, I know this continent. I've been from one end to the other for years. If your compass is accurate I can get us to Dolph."

"She's got a point," Zeke replied.

Famara winched then closed his eyes. One of the nurses came to his side then gave Zeke and Annette a disapproving look.

"Your friend needs to rest," she said in heavily accented English. "I must ask you to leave."

Famara touched the nurse's arm.

"It's okay," he said. He gave the compass to Zeke.

"I trust you with this," he said.

Zeke tucked the compass into his coat. "I've been paid. I never go back on a job. You'll get your book."

Annette bent over then kissed Famara on his cheek.

"I'll make sure Zeke is safe," she said with a smile. "Do not worry mon ami."

"I must insist that you leave," the nurse said.

Zeke and Annette left the room. They went immediately to Helmut. Zeke stood back letting Annette work her magic.

"Helmut, we'll need horses and provisions," she said.

"Of course," he replied. "My men are willing to help as well."

"Thanks but that won't be necessary," Zeke said. "We can handle this on our own."

Helmut's eyes narrowed. "Can you? It seems we have rescued you, and you have lost a book."

Zeke was about to answer when Annette stepped between them.

"We are so grateful for your help," she said. "How soon can we get our supplies?"

Helmut reached into his coat then took out a pad and pencil. He handed it to Annette.

"Just make me a list and you will have it immediately."

"Thank you, Helmut."

Helmut bowed. "My pleasure."

Helmut gave Zeke a sideways glance before walking away, shouting orders to his men as he left.

"I don't think that man likes me," Zeke commented.

"But he likes me, and that's all that matters," Annette said. "Stay close to me, Zeke of Freedonia. I'll take care of you."

Zeke tipped his hat then smiled. "I reckon you will."

27

Dolph followed Hansel down the frigid corridor, the cold made bearable by anticipation. The lights illuminating the corridor hinted at what was in store, their power far beyond anything lighting the streets of Paris. Hansel was his smartest investment by far, but the man was somewhat strange. In the beginning Dolph limited his access to the books, concerned about the eccentric man's behavior. He regretted his decision the further they descended into his mountain lair. What lay before him was pure brilliance.

The corridor opened into a large laboratory illuminated by rows of tubular lights on the ceiling. Benches ran from one end of the cavern to the other, crowded with sizzling, bubbling and gurgling flasks and beakers. The center of the room was filled with tables stacked with mechanical parts and devices in various state of development. The room was empty of any other people.

"Impressive," Dolph commented. "You've made tremendous progress."

Hansel turned, sharing an exaggerated grin.

"The books are the words of God himself. Every day another truth is revealed. I tell you Dolph this knowledge will change the world forever!"

"You did this all yourself?"

Hansel's grin transformed into a sly smile. "Not exactly."

He reached into his shirt then extracted a whistle. Pressing the whistle to his thin lips, his cheeks puffed out but there was no sound. The sound of metal striking rock echoed into the chamber; moments later a dozen mechanical creatures marched into the room.

"My God!" Dolph gasped.

"Meet my assistants, Herr Eriksson."

Automatons filed into the room, separating as they entered the cavern. Each metal man took a position at the lab tables then stood rigid.

"How many of these do you have?" Dolph asked.

"Thirty assembled," Hansel replied. "I have parts for at least twenty more. Their construction is similar to the cats but the wiring is more elaborate."

"What can they do?" Dolph asked.

"Very little," Hansel replied. His face took on a despondent look. "If I had privy to Carver's mind I could build an army!"

Dolph frowned at the mention of the Freedonian genius's name.

"I'm sure you can best any creation of that Negro," he said.

Hansel chuckled. "Your Prussian pride and European arrogance is getting the best of you, Herr Eriksson. I'm a scientist. I respect intelligence in whatever form it comes. I can't believe after seeing what I have produced with the knowledge contain in these Books that you still cling to such outdated notions."

"It's of no consequence," he said. "You will soon surpass Carver's advances."

Hansel caressed the book. "With this, I certainly will."

28

Zeke and Annette entered the alpine village close to dusk. Annette took the lead, urging her horse to a building that resembled an inn. Zeke sat up in his saddle, scratching his chin under his thick scarf.

"You sure these folks will be friendly?" he asked.

"The Swiss usually are," Annette answered. "Remember, you're my husband. That way we'll be less suspicious."

Zeke shared a mischievous grin. "That won't be easy to forget."

Annette narrowed her eyes. "Husband in name only. You are spoken for."

"I may be," Zeke replied. "But I ain't married."

Annette smiled. "Behave yourself, Zeke. We're on a mission."

Zeke could swear he noticed and extra sway in Annette walk as they entered the inn. A buxom woman with blond hair and deep brown eyes wiped the reception desk; she looked up at the two of them, unable to hide her surprise.

Bon jour, Madame," Annette said. "My husband and I seek lodging. Do you have rooms available?"

"Yes, yes we do!" the woman replied in French. "Voltaire! We have guests!"

A thin man with receding black hair and round spectacles entered the room. He looked at the two and was just as shocked as the woman.

"Welcome to our humble inn!" He rushed over to them, hugging them like lost family.

"Excuse my exuberance," the man said. "I am Voltaire Sabatini, and this is my lovely wife Brunhilda. It's not often we receive guests from Africa. As a matter of fact, I think this is a first!"

Annette smiled. "We are not from Africa, Voltaire. My husband and I are from New Haiti."

Voltaire clapped. "Even better! I have heard such wonderful things about New Haiti. Gave the French a black eye they did."

"Volty, they didn't come here to jaw with you," Brunhilda scolded. "They came for a room. Get their bags."

Voltaire frowned. "You're much stronger than me. You should get them."

"Voltaire!"

"Okay, okay!" Voltaire shuffled to their bags.

"This is the price you pay for marrying a beautiful woman," he said. "You become a slave to her whims."

Zeke looked at Brunhilda then held back a chuckle. The sprightly old man was about to pick up his bag but Zeke waved him away.

"I'll carry this one," he said.

"Of course, of course," Voltaire replied. The man looked as if he could barely stand with Annette's baggage alone.

"Come, I'll take you to your room."

"Give them our best!" Brunhilda called out.

"Of course my queen," he called back. "Of course!"

Annette and Zeke followed Voltaire upstairs then down a narrow hallway to a room at the end of the hall. He placed the bags down at the door then rummaged through his pockets for the key.

"Ha! Here you are!"

Voltaire opened the door then took their luggage inside. The room was modest yet cozy with a large rice bed filling the center. The window opposite the door gave an excellent view of the nearby mountains.

"It's lovely, no?" Voltaire asked.

"Very," Annette replied.

"I'll leave you two alone," he said. "Dinner will be served at 5:00 pm. I think we're having Wiener schnitzel tonight. Brunhilda is German. Her schnitzel is excellent!"

"I'm getting hungry just thinking about it!" Annette said.

Zeke went for his wallet but Voltaire waved him off.

"No tipping the owner!"

Voltaire skipped out of the room, leaving Annette and Zeke alone. Annette ambled to the window then took out Famara's compass.

"It's pointing to the mountains," she said.

"I was afraid of that," Zeke replied.

"We'll need to hire guides to take us up."

"We have enough gold," Zeke said.

"Then we go up tomorrow. Now get out."

Zeke looked dumbfounded. "What?"

'I said get out," Annette repeated. "I need to change."

Zeke grinned. "I thought we were man and wife."

Annette walked up to him, standing so close their noses almost touched.

"But we're really not and I need my privacy."

"It would have been easier just to get separate rooms," Zeke said.

"That would have been suspicious," Annette replied. "An unmarried woman and man traveling together? That's unheard of. Now go."

Zeke shrugged then headed downstairs. He waved absently at Brunhilda as he went outside then lit his pipe. He was missing Farama's company already. Traveling with Annette posed complications, the most being that he found her very attractive.

"What are you doing out here?"

Voltaire scampered up to him, wrapped in a heavy wool coat.

"It's too cold even for me, and I was born and raised here."

"It's not so bad," Zeke replied. "Besides, I needed some air."

Voltaire's eyebrows rose. "Ah! I think there is some friction between you and your wife, or maybe not enough friction?"

Zeke laughed. "You're a funny man, Voltaire. No, things between me and Annette are just fine."

"Except that she is not your wife," Voltaire said.

Zeke gave Voltaire a sideways glance.

"What makes you think that?" he asked.

"I am an old man, Zeke. Brunhilda and I have been married for twenty years. I know how married people are around each other.

There is no comfort between you, no familiarity."

"You got this one wrong," Zeke replied.

"Then where is her ring?" Voltaire asked. Zeke grinned.

"It doesn't matter to Brunhilda and me," Voltaire said. "We are very discreet. It comes with running an inn. Sometimes two people find themselves attracted to each other, and sometimes that attraction is not...how will I say...convenient. But we are not here to judge. Our purpose is only to provide comfortable lodging."

"Something tells me you have some experience in inconvenient relationships."

Voltaire laughed. "I do. When I first met Brunhilda she was days away from making the worst mistake of her life. She was about to marry the village butcher. The butcher! Could you imagine a beautiful woman as Brunhilda living such a life?"

Zeke could imagine Brunhilda as many things, but beautiful wasn't one of them.

"I was visiting her village with my wares. At the time I was a salesman of items from the exotic east. I saw her working in the fields and was immediately struck by her beauty. I had to make her mine!"

"I'm sure you did," Zeke said.

"Now I'm a realistic man, Zeke. I am not easy on the eyes, and I wasn't rich like I am now. But to Brunhilda I was a way out of her simple life."

Zeke lowered his pipe. "So you two ran off together?"

"Yes," Voltaire answered. "She did not love me at first, but as we traveled Europe together her heart finally gave in. We were married in a little chapel right outside of Venice. It was the happiest day of our lives."

"Voltaire!" Brunhilda shouted from inside. "Are you bothering our guests? The two of you come inside. Dinner will be ready soon!"

Voltaire grinned like a love-struck boy.

"See? How can you not love such a woman?"

Zeke put out his pipe. "How could you not?"

Brunhilda laid out an impressive spread, the aromas teasing Zeke's hunger. Annette made a late entrance dressed for dinner. Zeke held back an expletive, struck by her beauty.

"Lord give me strength," he whispered.

Voltaire held no such reservations.

"My God! An angel has descended upon us!"

Annette replied with a demur smile. "Thank you, Voltaire."

Brunhilda clapped. "A truly lovely vision! You are a lucky man, Zeke. Almost as lucky as my Voltaire."

"I agree with both of you," Zeke said.

They sat down to eat. Zeke wasn't familiar with anything on the table but it didn't matter. It was hot and it was there. Annette was more patient, complementing each dish as she tasted it. Brunhilda and Voltaire were enthralled by her. Zeke could see why Scofield sought her out as an agent. She could charm sugar out of salt.

After dinner they retired to the parlor for tea and pastries. A huge fire roared in the fireplace, warming the quaint room nicely.

"I was admiring the mountains from our room," Annette said.

"The Alps are lovely this time of year," Brunhilda replied.

"I'd like to visit them tomorrow," Annette replied. "It's been years since I skied and I'd like to dust off my skills."

A serious look passed between Brunhilda and Voltaire that didn't go unnoticed by Zeke.

"The mountains can be treacherous this time of year," Voltaire replied. "There are many sights in our village that are just as beautiful."

"But my heart is set on the mountains," Annette replied. "Surely there's a guide in the village who can take us to a safe slope."

"Oh dear!" Brunhilda said. "You better tell them, Voltaire. You're such a bad liar."

Voltaire cleared his throat. For the first time since their visit his face was serious as he gazed into the fire.

"The mountains are not safe," he said, his voice distant.

"They never were really. Accidents always happen and avalanches are a constant threat. One could get lost then freeze to death before being found. But these are dangers we are used to. They are dangers we grow up with. But the danger that lurks the mountains now is something like no one has seen."

He turned slowly to look at Annette and Zeke. "There is something in the mountains now. Something that kills indiscriminately. It is not an animal, because it does not eat what it kills. Its bite is unlike anything any of the hunters have seen. So we don't go into the mountains anymore, my friends. Neither should you."

Zeke leaned back in his chair, looking at Annette with serious eyes. There was no reason to keep up the façade; Voltaire knew they weren't married and Brunhilda would know soon. They would need someone's help to navigate the mountain roads and trails and their only chance would come from telling the truth, or at least as much as they could. Annette nodded.

"Well, folks, looks like we have a dilemma. Me and Miss

Annette need to go up into those mountains. We've been travelling a long time looking for something special to us and we're pretty much certain it's up there. So we're going, with or without a guide."

"But you can't!" Brunhilda shrieked. "You'll be killed!"

"Don't worry about us, Miss Brunhilda. Me and Miss Annette can handle ourselves." Zeke looked over to Voltaire.

"Now Voltaire, you know anybody crazy enough to lead us into those mountains?"

Voltaire looked back at Zeke with a stare that could punch a hole in a brick wall.

"Yes," he answered. "I am."

Brunhilda dropped her head into her hands then wailed. Zeke expected Voltaire to run to her side, but instead he remained in his seat, his eyes fixed on the fire. Annette went to her, hugging her close.

"You sure about this, Voltaire?" he asked.

"I'm sure, my friend. Deadly sure." Voltaire placed his teacup down on the table then stood.

"If you'll excuse me, I'll retire for the evening. It's been a long time since I've traveled into the mountains and I will need my rest. I know a man in the village that will supply us with everything we'll need. Goodnight, everyone."

Voltaire left the room. Brunhilda lifted her head, watching him walk away. She began crying again. Annette looked at Zeke, sympathy in her eyes.

"We'll make him stay," Zeke said.

Brunhilda shook her head hard. "He won't stay. Nothing anyone could do would stop him short of killing him."

"Why does he want to go?" Annette asked.

Brunhilda wiped away her tears with her napkin. She took a moment to compose herself before answering.

"My Voltaire has always doted on me, but there was another that he was just as close to; Stephan Gruber. Stephan and Voltaire were like brothers. When he wasn't with me, he was with Stephan.

But one day Stephan went into the mountains and never returned. Voltaire went after him..."

Brunhilda shuddered. "Voltaire went after him alone.

When he was late returning I ran to the village and the men formed a rescue team. They returned with my Voltaire. It was so terrifying. He was broken like a doll and bleeding everywhere. They also came back with Stephan's body. The next day a group of hunters when into the mountains seeking whatever had done this. None of them returned. Since that day no one has gone into the mountains. But Voltaire wanted to. He tried to convince someone, anyone to go. But they refused. Now you have come and he will go again. Don't let my Voltaire die, Zeke. Don't let him die!"

Zeke knelt before Brunhilda then took her hand.

"Ma'am, I promise you I'll do the best I can to bring Voltaire back alive. But you got to understand that he's determined to do this. We can only protect him so much. It ain't our intention to fight no type of creature. If we're lucky the only animals we'll have to deal with is the two-legged kind. But we'll do the best we can. That's all I can say."

"Thank you both," she said. "I get the feeling that whoever you are and whatever you do, you are good at it."

Brunhilda stood, bowed, and then hurried away. Annette and Zeke looked at each other, Annette's tight lips expressing her concern.

"Didn't expect that," Zeke said.

"I don't think he should go," Annette said. "He says he will guide us, but he might just lead us on a hunt for whatever that thing is in the mountains."

"I'll bet money that your German is behind all this, and whatever is killing these poor folks is something out those damn books," Zeke said.

"Whatever it is, we know what we must do," Annette said.

"We should retire as well. It will be long day."

Annette began walking to the stairs. Zeke sat in his chair.

"You're not coming?" she said.

"No, I think I'll bunk here on the couch," he replied.

"Don't be silly. Come upstairs."

Zeke smiled. "I best not, Annette. Circumstances being as they are, I couldn't guarantee I would behave in a gentlemanly manner tonight."

Annette smirked. "Good night then."

Zeke took one last sip of tea then left the parlor for the sitting room. The sofa was just long enough for his tall frame. He was taking off his boots when he heard someone approach. Annette entered the room with a blanket.

"I found this," she said.

Zeke reached for the blanket and she grasped his hand. When he pulled his hand away Annette fell onto his lap and then kissed him.

Zeke pulled away. "Annette, I don't..."

She pressed her fingers on his lips. "It's just a kiss. Don't make too much of it. If we succeed in retrieving Famara's book then we'll continue this discussion."

She kissed him again then stood.

"Goodnight, Annette," Zeke said.

Annette paused then spoke.

"You shouldn't have promised we would bring Voltaire back," she said.

"Pardon me?"

"You shouldn't have promised Brunhilda Voltaire would return. This is a vital mission. If Voltaire poses too much of a problem we might have to...deal with him."

Zeke glared at Annette. She was good without a doubt. He'd almost forgotten she was with them for a reason.

"This ain't no mission to me," he replied. "I'm here do to a job I was paid to do. I wasn't paid to kill someone if they make trouble. And like I told Brunhilda, I'll do my best to make sure her husband comes back."

Annette's eyes narrowed. "That might put us at odds, Zeke

Culpepper."

"It just might, Annette Bijou" Zeke replied.

A smile slowly came back to Annette's face. "I would hate that. I rather enjoyed our kiss."

She sauntered away.

Zeke shook his head as he fell back onto the couch then pulled the blanket over him.

"I'll be damned," he said out loud. "Looks like I'm going to have to keep an eye on Miss Annette as well."

He closed his eyes and tried to dream of Pauline.

* * *

Morning came too soon, entering the sitting room in lines of sunlight through the curtain edges. Zeke stretched then threw the blanket aside. He rubbed his eyes then sat up, a little disoriented. The dream of Pauline and the farm had been a bit too vivid, so much that he thought he was back home. But as he looked around the realization of his location sank in as did the seriousness of his situation.

"Good morning, Zeke."

Voltaire stood in the sitting room entrance, dressed for a trek in the mountain. The jovial countenance still not had returned to his face.

"Brunhilda is preparing breakfast for us," Voltaire said.

"Annette will be down soon. You must hurry. We will leave for the village as soon as we finish breakfast."

Zeke put on his boots. "Brunhilda told us why you're so anxious to go."

Voltaire looked away. "It was not her place."

"I'm glad she did," Zeke answered. "If I'm going to risk my life with somebody I need to know why they're risking theirs. And I got to tell you I'm not comfortable with your motives."

Voltaire stepped toward Zeke. "That thing killed my best

friend! That is my motivation!"

Zeke stood then placed his hands on his waist.

"What I need you to do is cool your heels," Zeke replied.

"You can't take your emotions into things like this. It will make you do stupid things that will get you...or us...killed. I can't get paid if I'm dead."

Zeke strolled past Voltaire, heading for the dining room. Voltaire took up beside him.

"What do you suggest?" Voltaire asked.

"You're the guide," Zeke replied. "We're depending on you to get us where we're going. But when it comes to the dangerous stuff Annette and I are in charge. You do everything we say exactly the way we say it. Otherwise I might have to put a bullet in your leg then send you home."

Voltaire cut his eyes at Zeke. "Would you? Annette wouldn't allow that!"

Zeke laughed. "Cause us some trouble and Annette is liable to put a bullet in your head."

Voltaire's expression did not change.

"Come," he said. "The women are waiting for us."

Breakfast waited at the table. Brunhilda's red eyes fell on Voltaire and a sob escaped her pursed lips. Annette studied him for a minute then shared a smile with Zeke.

"I see my companions are ready," she said.

Voltaire said nothing. He kissed Brunhilda then sat before his breakfast. Zeke sat beside Annette.

"You didn't come to my room last night," she whispered.

"I didn't know you were expecting me," he replied.

"I wasn't, but a woman can be hopeful."

Zeke smirked. "I think it's best to keep my distance. There's a woman waiting for me at home and I want to make sure I get back to her."

Annette chuckled. "I would never hurt you, Zeke."

"No you wouldn't, because I won't let you," Zeke replied.

Brunhilda sat at the table, her worried eyes lingering on Voltaire. They ate in silence, the clinking of silverware against glass the only sound. Brunhilda doted on Voltaire, refilling his plate when it was empty, pouring him for coffee when his cup was dry. It was a change of roles for them. She was about to fill his plate again when he raised his hand.

"Enough," he said. He stood the looked at Zeke and Annette.

"We are ready, no?" he asked.

Zeke wiped his mouth then stood. "I reckon we are."

Annette stood, finishing her coffee.

"We'll give you two time alone," she said.

Zeke followed her to the room, helping her with her gear.

"We should take all of it," she said. "Just in case Voltaire doesn't make it back."

"He'll make it back," Zeke said.

Annette froze, a frown forming on her face.

"I told you what we might have to do," she said.

"And I told you he'll make it back," Zeke replied.

He grabbed her bags then left the room. "And you wonder why I didn't come here last night."

When they returned downstairs Voltaire and Brunhilda stood at the door, Brunhilda crying softly on Voltaire's shoulder. Voltaire's hard countenance eased as he held her.

"I'll be fine, sweet flower" he said.

"I'll be so angry with you if you die," she said.

"Will you put flowers on my grave?" he asked.

"Of course, you fool," she replied.

They kissed long then finally broke apart. Voltaire turned to Zeke and Annette, an assuring smile on his face."

"Let's go, comrades," he said. "The mountains wait."

Zeke shivered as they followed Voltaire out into the cold morning. They circled the hostel to the outside stables. Zeke and Annette mounted their horses; Voltaire set out on foot.

"I'll get a mountain pony at the mountaineer's shop," he said. "I normally have no use for a horse."

"Are you a good rider?" Annette asked.

Voltaire grinned. "Good enough."

Annette cut her eyes at Zeke and he shrugged.

It took them a good hour to reach the mountaineer's cabin at the city's outskirts, a quaint home with smoke rising from the thin brick chimney. Five short but stout ponies chewed on a bale of snow rimmed hay. A tall man pushed another bale from a small barn, his breath freezing with each puff.

"Gunter!" Voltaire shouted.

The man's head jerked up, his eyes wide with surprise.

"Voltaire? What are you doing here?"

"Gunter, I'd like you to meet my friends Annette and Zeke," Voltaire answered.

Zeke and Annette rode to the fence then dismounted. Gunter shook their hands, his hard wrinkled face suspicious. He immediately looked to Voltaire.

"What's going on, Voltaire?" he asked.

"Zeke and Annette need to go into the mountains and I'm taking them," Voltaire said.

Gunter's face flushed red. "Are you crazy?"

Voltaire grinned at his friend. "It's been a long time, I know. I'll be a bit rusty but I'm sure I'll remember the trails."

"This has nothing to do with remembering the trails!"

Gunter shouted. He glared at Zeke and Annette. "Did he tell you why he hasn't been into the mountains?"

"Yes he did," Zeke answered.

The man's eyes narrowed. He turned back to Voltaire and immediately began yelling in a language Zeke couldn't understand.

"What the in the world is he saying?" he asked Annette.

"Some local dialect," Annette replied. "I can understand a word here and there. Something about going back home and letting these stupid Africans get killed on their own."

"I guess everybody in this village is not as nice as Voltaire and Brunhilda."

Annette smiled. "I guess not."

"I didn't come to argue with you," Voltaire said. "I came for ponies and supplies. Is that within your ability to supply?"

Gunter folded his thick arms across his chest and said nothing.

Voltaire walked up to the fence. "I know you need the money, Gunter."

"It's not about the money," the man replied.

Zeke had enough. He sauntered up to the fence, his hand heavy on his shotgun holster.

"Look, Gunter. It's very important my partner and I get up into those mountains. Now I'm willing to pay good gold to get there, but I plan to get those ponies and supplies one way or another."

"You're crazier than he is!" Gunter said.

"Maybe so," Zeke replied. "Now are you going to sell us what we need, or do we have to make this transaction more intense?"

"Meet me inside," Gunter said.

Gunter stomped away to the back of the cabin. Zeke and Annette followed Voltaire to the front entrance and then into the gear shop. Ropes, picks, and other mountain climbing equipment hung on the wall and filled the shelves. From a distance they seemed in pristine condition, but closer inspection revealed most had not been used in years. Gunter entered the back door then walked up to the counter.

"What do you need?" he asked.

Voltaire reached into his coat then pulled out a list. Gunter snatched the paper from his hand then shuffled back and forth between the shelves and the counters, bringing the equipment needed.

Voltaire looked over the equipment then nodded to Zeke.

"How much I owe you?" Zeke asked.

"Ten gold pieces," Gunter said.

"That doesn't look like a fortune worth of gear to me," Zeke said.

"Pay him," Annette said. "We must be on our way."

Zeke frown as he took out Famara's gold pouch then paid Gunter. The shopkeeper's eyes glistened and a smile came to his stoic face as Zeke dropped the gold into his hand.

Zeke and Voltaire gathered the gear then the three headed for the door.

"Stay away from the summits," Gunter called out.

The three of them turned back to Gunter.

"They lurk in the summits," he continued. "They like to attack from above. They use their weight to kill."

"You've seen them?" Annette asked.

"I've been into the mountains," Gunter confessed. "I go at least once a year. I've lost dozens of ponies trying to discover out how to stop them."

"You mean kill them?" Voltaire said.

"No, stop them," Gunter said. "They are not animals. This much I know. They are some kind of machine."

Zeke and Annette exchanged glances.

"Why would someone build such a thing?" Voltaire asked.

"To protect something," Zeke answered.

"I don't know what makes you think you can stop them, but I know bullets won't affect them."

Gunter reached under the counter the pulled out a double barreled shotgun, slamming it on the countertop.

"It won't kill them, but it slows them down," he said.

Zeke patted his shotgun. "I think this will do fine."

Voltaire took the shotgun. Gunter went to the shelves then came back with an ammunition belt loaded with shotgun shells. He came around the counter then draped the belt over Voltaire's shoulder.

"Thank you, my friend," Voltaire said.

"Thank me by coming back," Gunter said.

They followed Gunter out the back of the shop then into the stables. He saddled the tallest of the ponies for Voltaire then loaded two other ponies with provisions.

"You should make the first cabin by nightfall. You'll be safe until then. If you don't find what you're looking for there then God be with you. The second cabin will be a challenge on its own just because of the terrain. The trails are steep and dilapidated. And then there are the creatures. I don't suggest you go beyond the third cabin. There are no trails and you'll have to do a bit of mountain climbing. That is if you get beyond the second cabin."

Thank you, Gunter," Annette said.

Gunter opened the gate and the trio rode off. Zeke and Annette rode behind Voltaire as he led them out of the village and into the mountains. A few villagers peered out of their windows; some came outside waving Voltaire goodbye then making the sign of the cross.

By dusk they were climbing a steep road into the foothills. Gunter had apparently kept the road clear, making their journey to the first cabin relatively easy. The cabin fit into a small clearing on a steep slope, a building that hinted at more pleasant situations than the one the trio partook. A patch of winter grass and a snow covered haystack provided food for the horses and ponies and a fresh stack of wood rested against the cabin wall. They dismounted then walked to the cabin door. Voltaire unlocked the door. Annette gathered kindling while Voltaire and Zeke filled their arms with wood before following Annette inside. She prepared the huge fireplace as the men carried in the provisions. By the time they settled in the fire was building. Annette started a fire in the metal stove as well then brewed a pot of coffee.

They sat before the fire, sipping on coffee while savoring the aroma of lamb stew.

"The next cabin is a half a day's ride from here," Voltaire said.

"Which direction?" Zeke asked.

"North."

Annette stood. "Excuse us. Zeke?"

Voltaire nodded then stood and walked to the other side of the cabin. Annette took out Famara's compass. The device glowed brightly, pointing north.

"We're close it seems," she said.

"I have a feeling that if we're close to the book, we're close to whatever it is killing these folks."

"I agree. We'll have to be careful from here on out."

They ate a good meal then slept. Zeke dreamed of home, of his unkempt farm, the little church, and Pauline. When he woke the next morning it dawned on him the he'd been gone quite a long time. He wondered if Pauline worried about him, if she wondered if he was alive or dead. He made a point to send her a letter when they, or if they, returned.

They shared a breakfast consisting of the remaining stew then continued into the mountains. Voltaire rode in the lead again, but he held Gunter's shotgun across his lap. Zeke cradled his shotgun as well, loaded with his explosive shells. Annette's rifle rested across her legs, her eyes searching the brush and hills for any suspicious movement. The sun faded behind gathering clouds; by the time they viewed the cabin light snow gathered on their shoulders.

Zeke saw them first. They glided through the naked trees and rocks like fish down a familiar stream, barely making a sound. They resembled mountain cats, sleek tawny metallic bodies that moved with a stilted yet lifelike motion. He was about to shout a warning when a shot rang from behind him. Annette had her rifle to her shoulder, pulling back the bolt for a second shot. Voltaire began babbling in German as he raised his shotgun, anger full in his face. Zeke whipped his shotgun up. There was no use of him firing, they weren't close enough and the trees didn't give him a clear shot. Annette fired again; Zeke saw the bullet ricochet off the head of the cat-like machine to no effect.

"Get to the cabin!" Zeke shouted. Annette didn't need any urging. She galloped past him and Voltaire. Voltaire had climbed from his horse. He stood wide legged on the edge of the road, shouting at the approaching clockwork cats. A cat sprang into Voltaire's leg, sinking its metal teeth into his calf. Voltaire fired both barrels into it, the cat screeching as it shattered. The blast blew Voltaire off his feet and into his pony, which ran to the cabin behind Annette. The second cat ran to pounce on Voltaire.

"No you don't!" Zeke growled.

He fired two rounds into the cat's torso. There was a moment hesitation before both shells exploded, blasting the cat into pieces that showered Voltaire. Zeke rode up to Voltaire. He bled from numerous cuts but seemed to be okay.

"Now where's that third cat?" Zeke asked.

"Zeke!"

Zeke kicked his horse into action without looking. When he did look his heart fell into this stomach. The third cat chased Annette, gaining on her with every stride. There was no way he could reach her and he was out of range. He tried anyway, firing two shells that fell short, exploding on the trail. The cat leaped and Zeke closed his eyes, waiting for the scream.

It never came. When he opened his eyes Annette sat on her horse staring down at the complacent clockwork cat. Zeke raised his shotgun to shoot.

"No Zeke," Annette said. "You have to see this!"

Zeke rode up beside her. The cat sat motionless, ticking like a grandfather clock. Attached to its headpiece was Famara's compass.

"How in God's name did that happen?" Zeke asked.

"I don't know," Annette answered. The compass jumped out my coat then attached to the cat thing. As soon as it did the cat thing froze."

Zeke dismounted then walked up to the clockwork cat, his gun at the ready. He circled it slowly, studying it for anything odd.

"Maybe it will take us to where it came from," he said.

"How do we get it to do that?" Annette asked.

"Same way Famara does," Zeke said. He reached out then touched the compass. The cat stood on all fours then walked away. Zeke touched it again and it stopped.

"Here." He handed Annette his shotgun. "Just in case it changes its mind."

He trotted back to the wounded Voltaire. He helped the man to his feet then together they walked to the cabin.

"What are you waiting for?" Voltaire said. "Destroy that thing!"

"It's on our side now," Zeke replied. "It will take us where we need to go, I suspect."

Voltaire pulled away from him. "Those things are evil!"

Zeke pushed his hat back. "It's a machine. It does what it's told to do. Right now we're telling it what to do."

Voltaire's eyes narrowed. "How do I know you haven't controlled them all along? How do I know that they are protecting something for you?"

"You're talking crazy now," Zeke answered. "Why in the …I mean why on earth would I have my own machines attack me? Come on, now. We're wasting time."

They carried Voltaire into the cabin. Zeke built a fire while Annette tended Voltaire's wounds. Once the fire was made Zeke sat their provisions by Voltaire.

"We have to get going," Zeke said.

"Shouldn't we wait until morning?" Annette asked.

Zeke shook his head. "We have to make a run tonight. Once whoever sent those things realized the toys ain't coming back they're going to send more and be on guard. That cat outside will take us to their hideout."

Voltaire sat up. "I'm going."

"No, you're staying here," Zeke said. "You've done enough. I promised Brunhilda I'd bring you home safe and I'm keeping that promise."

He cut his eyes at Annette and she smiled slightly.

"But I can help!" Voltaire said.

"You've done what you came to do," Zeke said. "Now I ain't taking no more lip. You stay here and rest. Me and Miss Annette got work to do."

Zeke waited for Annette to grab her gear. They left the cabin then corralled the horses.

"You think we'll find the hideout before dark?" Annette asked.

"We better," Zeke answered. "Or it's going to be a mighty cold night. Them clock cats are windups, which mean they can only travel so far. So I'm guessing wherever they came from is close." Annette mounted her horse while Zeke strolled to the dormant clock cat. He touched the compass and the cat rose on all fours then trotted down the trail. Zeke ran to his horse. They followed the machine cat up the mountain, racing against the approaching darkness.

The clockwork cat kept to the trail for the first hour then veered right into the wooded hill. The brush was too thick for the horses, so Zeke and Annette grabbed what they could carry then followed the machine into the steep slopes. It was hard going; Zeke had to pull Annette up a number of steeper climbs.

"I need to rest," Annette finally said.

Zeke looked about then spotted a clump of tree.

"Follow me."

They worked their way to the trees then sat among them, huddled close for warmth.

"This is nice," Annette said.

Zeke's eyebrows rose. "Really? Kind of cold to me."

Annette laughed. "So how did you get in this line of work, Ezekiel Culpepper?"

Zeke took out a pocket knife then cut a branch from a nearby tree.

"I grew up on a farm. Shooting was like breathing. I always had a good eye. According to my daddy that was the only good thing about me."

"I take it you two did not get along," Annette said.

Zeke began whittling the branch. "That's an understatement. About the time I was sixteen I had to leave the farm. Either that or we were going to kill each other. I wandered about for a while, picking up odd jobs here and there. One day I looked up and I was in New Haiti, New Orleans to be exact."

"I'm from New Orleans!" Annette said.

"I suspected so. You got that blues thing in your voice. Anyway, I knocked about there but realized I wasn't going to find a good living there either. So one day I walked up to the Haitian army barracks and enlisted."

"Weren't you too young?"

"That's what they said until they saw me shoot," Zeke said.

"They signed me up then sent me straight to the Borderlands."

Annette interrupted his whittling when she snuggled closer to him.

"You said you fought in the Reunion War," she said.

Zeke nodded. "I was on leave in New Orleans when the Americans invaded Virginia. As soon as I got word I started packing my things to head back to Freedonia. But the Haitians wouldn't release me. I learned later that they planned on joining the war but they were waiting for the right time. Cut it pretty close, too. The Americans were marching through Tennessee with their eyes set on Atlanta when we were shipped up the Mississippi to invade America from the Midwest. Caught everybody off guard. The war didn't last too much longer after that. By the time we reached Pennsylvania the papers were signed and I was on my way back home."

Zeke inspected his work then looked at Annette.

"So how did a pretty woman like you end up the toast of France?"

"My father was a prominent general in the Haitian Army. My mother was the daughter of a dignitary with close ties to the king. We traveled to France frequently despite the cold relations between the countries. When my grandfather became enemies of the king we were labeled enemies as well."

"I don't think this story is going to end well," Zeke said.

"It doesn't," Annette said. "My grandfather was arrested and hanged, as was my father. My mother and I managed to escape to New Orleans. We lived there for a few years but we were still in danger. So we finally came to France. By then I was singing in public so I continued in Paris. To my surprised I became a star."

Annette paused to take a drink of water. "When my mother died I lost all desire to perform. I bought a villa in Lorraine and planned to live the rest of my life in semi-solitude when John Scofield contacted me on behalf of Freedonia."

"So why did you decide to serve? You ain't Freedonian?"

Annette shrugged. "I needed to be needed. Besides, part of my job is to keep an eye on the Haitians. I owe them for ruining my life. They will pay one day."

Zeke stopped whittling. "How you feeling?"

"Much better now," Annette said.

"We best get back to it then."

The trees thinned as they climbed higher; after another hour they walked among bare rock and snow. Zeke was not happy at all. They were exposed to anyone with bad intentions and a good rifle. He kept his eye on the cat until it disappeared. They hurried as much as they could after it then found themselves peering over a ledge. The cat sauntered up to a small cave entrance then sat.

Zeke took out his shotgun as Annette readied her rifle.

"You ready?" he asked.

Annette nodded.

The two of them scrambled over the edge, sprinting across the narrow trail. As soon as they reached the cave the clockwork cat proceeded inside. The darkness of the entrance gave way to a muted light. Zeke peered upward; metal coated cables connected a series of light running the length of the tunnel. The tunnel sloped downward, expanding as they proceeded deeper into the mountain. As the tunnel came to a large opening the clockwork cat halted.

The room rang with the sounds of metal work. Zeke and Annette peeked inside, marveling at the sight. Below them was a robotic assembly line. Automatons of various shapes and sizes worked on a myriad of projects. Some built other robots, while others hammered metal plates into various shapes. Another group of metal men labored in a lab environment, monitoring bubbling beakers and flasks, adjusting burners and adding ingredients. In the center of all the activity was a short man draped in a dingy lab coat, his arms cradling a large, leather bound book. Dolph stood beside the man.

"So what do we do now?" Annette asked.

"I have a plan," Zeke said. "Give me your rifle."

Annette handed Zeke the rifle. Zeke check the rifle to make sure it was loaded, and then drew a bead on the man in the lab coat.

"Zeke, no!" Annette said.

Zeke fired, the room echoing with the shot. The man's head jerked back then he crumpled to the floor. He swung the gun the left but Dolph was gone. The robots rose in unison then ran toward them.

"What kind of plan is this?" Annette asked.

"The best I could come up with," Zeke replied.

Zeke snatched the compass from the clockwork cat and the cat collapsed to the stone floor.

A bullet ricocheted off the wall near his head. Zeke and Annette ducked for cover. Zeke slid the rifle back to Annette.

"I'm going to make a move," he said. "You keep an eye out for him."

Annette nodded then brought the rifle to her shoulder.

Zeke dashed forward. Dolph fired nicking his shoulder. Annette fired immediately afterwards.

"I got him sighted!" she shouted.

Zeke didn't hear her. A mass of robots trudged up the ramp, their arms lifted over their heads.

"Here we go!" Zeke said.

Shotgun blasts echoed throughout the chamber. Robots shattered before Zeke, the explosive shells taking their toll. Behind him Annette and Dolph dueled from a distance, exchanging rifle fire from the darkness. Zeke's boots crunched over metal parts and quivering robots as he blasted his way down into the main chamber. The books lay open before him on a wide table. As he tried to reach them Dolph unleashed a torrent of gunfire. Zeke ducked under the nearest table.

"Annette!" he shouted. "Some cover fire if you don't mind."

There was no answer. An empty feeling hit Zeke's gut. He checked his ammo; he had two explosive shells remaining. He looked up to where Annette should be but saw no movement.

"It seems your companion has suffered a terrible fate," Dolph shouted. "You are at a disadvantage, Freedonian."

"Don't think you're doing much better," Zeke shouted back. "You got a dead scientist and a bunch of broken up mechanical men. Why don't you just let me take the books and be on my way?"

"I'm afraid I can't do that," Dolph replied. "But we can be gentlemen about this. I'll allow you to retrieve your friend's body and 'be on your way' as you say."

A shot rang out.

"Shiesse!" Dolph said.

Zeke sprang up then fired two explosive shells in the direction of Dolph's voice. The shells exploded against the rock, causing a minor avalanche.

"Ahhh!"

Zeke sprinted to the table. He jumped over the dead scientist's body as he holstered his shotgun. Once at the table he slammed the books closed then tucked them under his arms. Then he ran back up the ramp. Annette lay on the ground, barely holding her rifle. Blood ran from her stomach as she tried to smile.

"I'll slow you down," she managed to say. "Go, take the books."

"I'm not leaving you," he said.

"You can't carry the books and me," she said.

"No I can't," he replied.

Zeke set the books down. He ran back down into the lab to the table where the books rested then searched through the wreckage until he found what he was looking for; a satchel large enough to hold both books. He ran back to Annette. He placed the books in the satchel then tied the satchel to the mechanical cat's back. He reattached the compass to the cat and it reactivated, its eyes becoming beams of light.

"Now let's do something about that wound."

Zeke tore his shirt then made a makeshift bandage. Once he stopped the bleeding he cradled Annette in his arms then carried her out the cave, the clockwork cat following like a docile pet. The journey down the mountain was a precarious ordeal but he managed to get them both to their horses. He placed Annette on his horse then climbed on behind her. They rode down the path as fast as he could muster, reaching the cabin just before dark. When he entered the cabin carrying Annette Voltaire jumped to his feet.

Voltaire's smile transformed into a glare when he saw the clockwork cat enter behind them. He ran to his shotgun.

"No, Voltaire," Zeke said. "Help me get Annette to the bed."

Together they gently carried Annette to the cot. Voltaire looked at her wound then grimaced.

"This is bad," he said. "We need to get her to the village as soon as possible."

"It's almost dark," Zeke said.

"So we must hurry," Voltaire answered.

They changed Zeke's makeshift bandage with bandages packed by Gunter then hurried to their horses. Voltaire made a wide berth around the clockwork cat, his angry eyes locked on the thing. Zeke saw his reaction. He walked over to the automaton then disengaged the compass. He then went to Voltaire, handing him his shotgun.

"Go ahead," Zeke said.

Voltaire snatched the gun from his hand. He immediately pumped three rounds into the thing, grinning as each round exploded. He handed the gun back to Zeke.

"Thank you, my friend," he said. "Thank you."

They arrived in the village hours after dark. They were forced to walk, both of them carrying torches to light the way.

Annette managed to stay in the saddle despite her wound.

"Gunter! Gunter!" Voltaire shouted.

A light appeared in the window of Gunter's cabin. Moments later the shopkeeper stepped into the darkness with a kerosene lamp then shuffled up to them.

"Voltaire, what are you doing here this late? Don't you know those things...?"

"They are destroyed, every last one of them," Voltaire said.

"But our friend is hurt. She needs a doctor."

Gunter's eyes widened when he saw Annette.

"Come!" he said.

He led them to his small bedroom. Zeke eased Annette into the bed as Gunter shuffled off then returned with fresh bandages.

"I've get Victor," he said.

Zeke carefully changed Annette's bandages. She winced then looked at him with desperate eyes.

"Hang in there, little lady," he said. "You gonna be alright."

Zeke sat beside her holding her hand while Voltaire paced back and forth. Moments later the back door of the cabin flew open; Gunter and Dr. Victor Weismann rushed inside. Dr. Weisman wore a heavy coat over his sleeping clothes. His annoyed expression faded when he saw Annette.

"Stand aside," he ordered. Zeke stood and the doctor took his place.

"I know this woman," he said. "This is Annette Bijoux."

He removed Zeke's bandages to look at her wound.

"She's been shot! How did this happen?"

"We can talk about that later," Zeke said. "Can you help her?"

The doctor frowned at Zeke. "Of course I can. It's a bad wound, but she'll be fine. I have to take out the bullet. Will you assist me, Gunter?"

"Of course," the shopkeeper replied.

Annette handled the pain well as the doctor extracted the bullet. He disinfected the wound with spirits then set about stitching it. Voltaire retreated to the other side of the shop, unable to watch. Zeke hovered over the two during the entire procedure.

The sight brought back old memories of battlefield hospitals and loss comrades.

The doctor leaned back in his chair then wiped his sweaty forehead.

"She will be fine," he said. "But she will need much rest."

"How much rest?" Zeke asked.

"At least two weeks," Victor replied.

"Zeke, you'll have to take the books back to Famara," Annette replied. "Two weeks is too long for you to wait."

"Nope," he replied. "Can't leave you here among strangers."

"She's not among strangers," Voltaire replied. "You and Annette are like family to Brunhilda and I. And the village will be most gracious now that you have rid our mountains of those metal monsters."

Zeke rubbed his chin. "You sure you'll be okay?"

Annette managed to smile. "You forget who I am."

Zeke smiled back. "I guess you will."

Zeke sat by Annette's side until she slept. Gunter made a bunk for him and he fell into it with relish. He closed his eyes, his mind filled with the image of Pauline and his farm. He'd been gone long enough. It was time to collect and go home.

29

Dolph coughed as he stumbled through the black smoke filling the cave. He worked his way toward the work bench, hoping the damned Freedonian had not managed to get the books. His painful journey was in vain; the books were gone. He stepped over Hansel's body, taking a brief moment to gaze upon the dead scientist. He shook his head; such a waste. There was so much promise in the man, despite his eccentricity. He coughed hard, the smoke growing denser with every second. He couldn't see the entrance; his only choice was to find the exit to the rear of the cave.

Dolph tied a handkerchief around his mouth and nose then crawled below the smoke, clambering over robot parts and other debris to the supply entrance. He shuffled down the cold corridor, the wind whipping about him driving the smoke away. His way cleared and he exited to the mountainside. Hansel's steam car was before him, but there was no way he could navigate it down the narrow trails in darkness. Instead he lit the boiler then huddled near the engine to warm himself.

He'd failed again. Without the books the future of his family lay in shambles. He'd violated his orders knowing that he could use the books' knowledge to lift his family to riches, but now for the second time in months the damned African and his Freedonian friend had laid his plans to ruins.

Dolph was out of options. There was only one thing to do. If he was lucky he could regain a portion of his respect and dignity;

if not he would spend the rest of his life in prison and his family would be forever humiliated. He curled up tighter near the engine. His first priority was to survive the night. In the morning, if there was a morning, he would play his final hand.

Dolph woke to bright light which stung his eyes, the rising sun generous with its light but not its heat. His bones cracked and his joints ached as he pulled himself away from the steam car's bonnet then knelt beside the car to re-light the boiler. As the boiler heated and built pressure Dolph returned to the burned out lab, salvaging whatever valuables he could find. The engine howled its readiness and Dolph returned, dropping his loot into the passenger's seat. Then he began the dangerous drive down the narrow road leading to the base of the mountain. To his relief Hansel had widened the road to accommodate the steam car. Nevertheless, to someone not familiar with the road it was a difficult drive. Dolph exhaled as he reached foothills, increasing his speed. He would go to Italy then take the train back to Prussia. An airship would be faster but he needed time to heal and to think. Dolph drove the entire day, reaching the Swiss-Italy border at dusk. The town resting on the border mountains was already asleep, the windows of the chalets dark. Dolph had no intentions of spending the night outside. He parked the steam car at the outskirts then trudged through the snow covered fields for the refuge of the first barn he reached. He bundled into a pile of hay then fell to sleep as soon as his head settled in the warm straw.

"Get up! Get up!"

Dolph's Italian was weak, but the pitchfork made the farmer's mood clear. He held up his hands as he sat up.

"I meant no harm," he said. "I just needed a place to sleep."

"This is no hotel, Prussian, Get out now."

Dolph stood then backed away toward the barn door.

"Forgive me," he said.

Dolph kicked the farmer in the gut. The farmer dropped the pitchfork as he collapsed onto his knees. Dolph kicked the man in the face, sending him onto his back. He picked up the pitchfork then stabbed the farmer in the neck.

His anger ebbed with the farmer's life. He tossed the pitchfork aside then strode from the barn, ignoring the worried voice of the farmer's wife as she ran to the barn. The sound of the hissing steam car muffled her screams as she discovered her husband's body; he was well on his way by the time she emerged from the barn with blood on her hands.

The next town was more fruitful. There was a train depot and a bank where Dolph was able to convert his gold into currency. He visited the local haberdashery for new clothes then bought a first class ticket to Prussia. He studied every face in the station as he boarded the train; worried that word would reach the town of the farmer's death before his departure. The train pulled away from the station on time and Dolph let go of his vigilance. He kept his mind clear during the long journey, pushing away any thoughts of his recent failure. He was going home. He needed time with his wife and his family, time to contemplate his next moves. He would eventually have to face the High command, but he would stall as long as he could. His plan could still work. It would work.

30

The small Bavarian town was almost as good as seeing home. Zeke rode down the narrow streets, exhausted, relieved and triumphant. He patted the satchel hanging on the side of horse, the books secure. Mission accomplished.

The townsfolk greeted him with a range of attention, from curious glares to welcoming smiles. A group of children followed him from a distance, whispering, pointing and laughing. A stern looking constable finally approached him.

"You are Famara's friend?" he said in stilted English.

"That I am," Zeke replied. "You wouldn't know where I could find him, would you?"

"He's at Helmut's home," the constable replied. "I will take you there."

He followed the constable to the center of town. Helmut's home was near the city hall, a quaint building with empty flower holders under the windows. The constable knocked on the door as Zeke hitched his horse then slung the satchel holding the books over his shoulder.

Helmut met him at the door, his eyes widen.

"Where is Annette?" he asked.

Zeke smirked. "I'm happy to see you, too. Miss Annette had to stay behind for a spell. Don't worry, she's in good hands."

Zeke stepped around the disappointed burgermeister. Famara rose from a chair before a small table, his eyes expectant.

Zeke sauntered up to the table then placed the satchel down.

"Here you go," Zeke said.

A wide smile creased Famara's face. He opened the satchel then extracted the books one at time. His smile grew wider as he confirmed the authenticity of the tomes.

"You've done well, horro," he said.

Zeke pulled up a chair then sat.

"Is Annette okay?" Famara asked.

"That pretty lady is as tough as nails," Zeke answered. "Ol' Dolph had a backup laboratory. We took it down, but Annette was wounded kind of bad in the process. A local doctor patched her up good but she needed a rest. She insisted I get a move on and get you these books. Like I told her boyfriend' –he looked at Helmut then winked- 'she's in good hands."

"As I said, good job, horro."

Zeke folded his hands behind his head. "I don't know about this horro stuff, but we have business to attend to."

Famara nodded. "I can pay you now, but there is another option."

Zeke smirked. "I'm listening."

"Come to Timbuktu with me. I'll need your protection since I'm still recovering, and the Elders can be much more generous than I can."

Zeke rubbed his chin. "I suspect me going to Timbuktu has nothing to do with protecting you or a bigger payday."

"It doesn't," Famara admitted. "Come to Timbuktu, Zeke. You deserve to know why the books are so important."

"What about Annette? She had a hand in this as well."

Famara grinned. "Annette answers to people who need not know what is at stake at this point."

"So you don't trust Annette and you trust me?" Zeke asked.

"Your motivations are simple," Famara replied. "But I think

there is more to you than even you suspect."

"I think you're seeing too much," Zeke replied. "Most people do. All I want to do is get back home to my farm and my woman."

Famara leaned forward. "It's a simple choice. I can pay you a small sum now, or a much larger sum in Timbuktu. So what do you say, Zeke? Will you accompany me?"

Zeke played with his cross. "Always wanted to go to Africa. You sure those Elders will spring for more gold?"

Famara's smile widened. "I'm positive."

Zeke extended his hand and they shook.

"So when do we leave?"

31

Dolph sat shackled in the dank prison cell, awaiting his meeting with the high command. He was stoic in his demeanor, but inside his emotions churned. He knew his return would not be taken lightly, but he was surprised how he had been treated. His family was well respected in Prussia and he deserved much better consideration because of it. Instead he'd been handled like a common soldier, arrested immediately when he contacted his uncle. The soldiers had come directly to his home, dragging him from his bedroom to a prison wagon, his wife and children looking on with terror in their eyes. His only hope was that Hans would be part of the court martial proceedings. To be dishonorably discharged from the army would be an insult from which he and the family would never recover.

His guards came for him that afternoon after he finished his sparse meal. They brought him a fresh uniform in respect to his rank. He dressed quickly then followed them outside. It was a cool spring day in Prussia; remnants of winter's snow clung to the sidewalks and tree trunks. He took a deep breath, filling his lungs with the clean, crisp air. The guards were polite despite his current state, opening the door to the wagon as he entered.

The ride to the Reichstag was shorter than he hoped. The guards escorted him inside the imposing building, directly to the court martial chamber. To his dismay Himmler and Reuters sat on the court. Hans Backer was present, but so were three other generals whom he did not recognize. He would have to play his final card as soon as possible before his trial had a chance to reach deliberations. This court would surely send him to prison if he waited.

One of the unknown generals stood to speak.

"Field Marshal Dolph Erickson, I am General Anton Dresner, auditeur of the court of honor. You are here today to face court martial charges due to insubordination. How do you plead?"

"Herr Generals, before I plead I would like to take a moment to explain my actions."

"There's nothing to explain," Claus cut in. The grin on his face showed he was enjoying himself.

"As a member of a respected family he is allowed a statement before we go on," Hans said. He clearly was not happy with Dolph, but he continued to perform his family obligations.

"Respect or nepotism?" Claus asked.

"Both," Hans replied.

"Enough," Anton said. "You have the floor, Field Marshal."

"Thank you, general. As all of you know my position with the army is purely scientific. It was hoped that my tenure would produce such information that would be of advantageous use of the military. A few years ago I discovered the existence of a collection of books which could possibly hold technical knowledge that could advance Prussian science far beyond any country in the world, even Freedonia."

Claus leaned back in his chair then smiled. Let the fool hang himself, his expression read. Hans shook his head, silently warning Dolph to stop. Dolph looked away from him. This was his final gambit.

"For the past four years I have collected these books and financed with my own money research to develop the knowledge of these books into practical application. A few months ago I was informed by our allies that there was another book available in North Africa. I sent an airship to assist them."

"The airship that was destroyed," Claus added.

Dolph ignored his nemesis. "After the failure of the mission General Hans insisted I take some time off to contemplate my actions. I could not. I believe what these books possess is so important that I defied his orders and personally set out to obtain the book. It was then I discovered that there were two books available. I also discovered there were other forces attempting to obtain the books. That could not be allowed."

Anton leaned back into his chair, clearly unhappy.

"It's a good story, but it has nothing to do with the fact that you disobeyed orders, jeopardizing your rank as well as the reputation of General Hans."

Dolph expected such a response. "I realize you and others are skeptical of the knowledge of the books. How could something so advance come from Africa? We forget that Egypt was once the most advanced civilization on this Earth. The Greeks and Romans looked upon them with reverence and awe. The knowledge possessed in these books precedes Egypt. It is from the books that one of my scientists was able to produce this."

Dolph reached into his pocket then took out the scarab box.

"May I approach?" he asked.

The general nodded. Dolph walked forward then placed the box on the table. He pressed a button on the side of the box. The lid raised; there was a tiny spark then an image floated from the inside.

"What is this?" the general asked, his voice filled with wonder.

"It is a projection box," Dolph replied. "What you see is what is happening outside these doors. I placed a device in the courtyard which records the images then projects them to this box."

Even Claus was fascinated. Hans gave him an assuring smile.

"What else do your labs hold?" the general asked.

Dolph closed the box. "Unfortunately both labs were destroyed by those seeking to take the books."

"Do you know who they are?"

"The Freedonians are definitely involved," Dolph replied.

"I believe they are trying to protect their technological advantage over the rest of the world. The other group is a mystery to me. They are definitely African, but from where they operate I don't know."

"Maybe another country using the Africans as cover?" the general surmised. "I suspect England or maybe the Belgians."

Claus stood, his face twisted. "Are you actually buying this drivel? Dolph appears with a charlatan trick and you fall into his hands?"

"Sit down, general," Anton said. "Your position on this tribunal is precarious at this moment."

Claus shoved his chair away. "You can save your threats. I refuse to be a part of this travesty. This fool has fouled the reputation of his family and himself and is about to take the rest of you with him. I expected better."

Claus stormed out of the room. Dolph lowered his head to hide his smile. The other generals sat quietly until Claus exited the room, slamming the door behind him.

"Do you know where the books may be?" the general asked.

"I'm not exactly sure, but my allies could give us an idea. If I could contact them I would know soon."

"What do you need?" another general asked.

"My allies can mobilize hundreds of fighters for the right incentive," Dolph replied. "However I would feel better if Prussians were present. I would also need airships."

The generals murmured amongst themselves.

"Will you excuse us for a moment, General?" Hans said.

"Of course," Dolph replied. He saluted then strode from the room, a smile forming on his face. When the generals sent for him he was confident he'd convinced them.

"You'll have your airships," the general said. "And you'll have your pick of men."

"Thank you general!" Dolph exclaimed. "Thank you all."

"Thank Hans," the general replied. "He believes in you despite your failures."

Dolph turned to leave the room.

"One more thing Herr Eriksson," the general said.

Dolph turned about. "Yes sir?"

"As far as the generals here are concerned we have no knowledge of what you are about to do. If you fail you will bear this burden alone. Do you understand?"

Dolph cleared his throat. "Yes general. I understand."

"Good luck, Dolph," Hans said.

"Thank you, Hans," Dolph replied.

Dolph hurried from the room. He would have to assemble another team, men who had as much at stake as he. He had this one last chance to redeem his reputation and his family's fortune. He would not fail.

32

Menna secured her rifle over her shoulder then tightened the shoulder strap across her chest. She inspected her revolvers, making sure each was loaded before returning them to her holster then snapping them in place. Her daggers rested in her waist belt with four smaller knives pressed against her thighs and calves. Her breath fogged through her shesh as she gazed one last time on the looming mansion before her. Weak moon light did little to expose the details of the house, but Menna needed none. She spent two days studying the compound, noting every possible entrance and exit while marking the patterns of the guards disguised as farm workers. Whoever this Annette Bijoux was, it was much more than a retired entertainer.

Her reluctant sources in England pointed her to this woman. Apparently she assisted Famara Keita on his quest to retrieve a book for his masters. It was not the book he stole from her brother; apparently there was more than one tome and they had a habit of disappearing. That was no concern to her. She was here to find the horro then bring him or evidence of his death back to her kel. The book was insignificant.

A bell rang, signaling the eighth hour and time for the shift change of the guards. Menna sprinted to the tree line then worked her way to the rear of the house, keeping close to the trees and hedges. The rear of the home was the most heavily guarded but was also the closet to the guest rooms. As she reached her destination a solitary light came into view on the second floor. Annette was in her room, preparing for bed most likely. It was good for her; if she remained inside she would survive the night.

Menna broke away from the trees, sprinting toward the house. She had five minutes to reach the structure before the replacement guards reached the rear of the building. She leaped the low fence separating the fallow fields from the grounds then cursed as he heard voices in the distance. She ran across the paved path to the stables, reaching into her coat then extracting two black handled daggers. As the guards emerged to her left she dropped to her knees then threw the daggers. One dagger struck its mark, plunging into the unfortunate guard's neck. The second dagger was less successful, bouncing off the brick wall when the startled man stumbled away from his dying friend.

"Martin?" he said.

Menna was halfway to the man before he turned toward her. He tried to raise his rifle but she kicked it from his hand then grabbed it in mid-air. Menna smashed the rifle butt into the man's mouth and he fell to his knees. Her left hand covered his mouth before he could cry out; his eyes clinched as she drove a dagger into his heart. Menna ran to the house as the man collapsed to the pavement.

The incident cost her precious time. She climbed the wall then jimmied open the first window she reached. It was not her preference, but she needed to be inside when the other guards discovered their dead comrades. She eased the window down then crept to the stairs. There were no guards in the expansive foyer, or any on the stairs. Apparently the mistress of the house felt safe inside her home. It would be her undoing.

Menna rushed up the stairs to the top floor. She burst into the first room, finding it empty. The second room gave the same results. The excited voices of the guards reached her as she entered the third room. When she stepped out into the hallway she was greeted by the sight of a petite brown skinned woman draped in a nightgown holding two machetes.

"Ki sa ki se sa a?" Annette blurted.

Menna threw her dagger which Annette deftly batted away with a machete. Then she attacked, the machetes blurring like hummingbird wings. Menna stumbled away, stunned by the speed and precision of Annette's assault. The rifle strap snapped as a machete grazed her chest; Menna caught the gun as she spun away from another machete strike. She raised the rifle then fired, more to slow down her attacker than to strike her. Annette dodged to the side before resuming her attack, knocking the rifle aside while stabbing at Menna's stomach. Menna twisted to her left, avoided the blade. She struck Annette in the chin with the rifle butt and the woman fell back against the wall.

Menna raised the rifle to shoot then cursed. The barrel had been damaged by the machete blow. She threw the rifle at the stunned Annette; the woman blocked it with both machetes. Menna raised her revolvers too late. Annette was on the attack again. She knocked one of the guns from Menna's hand, almost severing her fingers. Menna spun with the blow then fired the second handgun. Annette winced as the bullet creased her waist.

"Mademoiselle Bijoux!"

Guards piled into the hallway from the stairs, their faces twisted in shock and anger. Menna emptied her gun as Annette dropped to the floor for cover and the men scattered.

Menna grinned as she turned then ran. With a takouba she would have stood her ground. The French woman was impressive, but Menna was better. Her knives were no match against such a skilled person, and now she was outnumbered. She'd come for Famara and it was obvious he was not in the house. That meant he was on his way back to Timbuktu.

Menna crashed through the window then slid down the roof. She landed awkwardly on the hard pavement, bruising her ankle. She loaded her revolver as she limped toward the tree line. As she disappeared into the foliage she turned and fired a few more rounds for good measure. They would be cautious now, giving her the time she needed to locate her horse and be on her way. Her search for the horro was over. It was time to go home and settle the score.

33

The French airship Chant De La Vie hovered over the shimmering asphalt, its blades stirring dust devils upon the landing pad. Zeke and Famara hid their faces with cloth from their turbans as they hurried from the terminal. Zeke glanced about at his surroundings in wonder. He'd always imagined Africa as steaming jungle and half-naked savages, but what he witnessed was a stark contrast. Mali was an arid land of pastels accented by brightly dressed dignified people who looked at him just as curiously as he looked at them. Another robed man waited for them, holding the reins of two magnificent horses.

"After so many years among the Ihaggaren I prefer camels," Famara said. "But I feel horses would be best for you."

"You figured right," Zeke answered. He inspected his horse before mounting.

"This is a good horse," Zeke commented. "Damn good.

"The Sokoto breed the best horses," Famara replied.

"In Mali?"

"In the world," Famara answered with a wink.

They galloped away from the terminal and through the stone gates of Timbuktu. The city's wide avenues were clean yet dusty, bustling with brown skin folks going about their business. They rode to the center of the city to a nondescript building with an elaborately carved door. They hitched their horses then walked to the door. Famara's hand went absently to the satchel holding book before knocking. The door eased open, revealing a young man with wisps of hair on his chin.

"Famara!" the boy exclaimed. "It is good to see you again."

"Hello, Amadou. It is good to be seen."

Amadou glanced at the satchel and his face became serious.

"Come. The Elders are waiting."

The boy led them into the building through a narrow hallway then into a round central room. Eight elderly men and women sat in a circle on silk cushions. Young men and women served them tea and pastries. They looked in unison at the two men, acknowledging their presence with curt nods. Zeke followed Famara into the center of the circle as the servers exited the room.

"Honored Elders," he said. "I have returned with the books."

He opened the satchel and extracted the books. A thin woman with short grey hair and penetrating eyes gestured him to her. He went to her, knelt, and then opened the book. She studied it, turning the pages gingerly.

"It is as he says," she announced. "These are the last."

"Who is this?" one of the elders asked.

Famara returned the book to the satchel and returned to the center of the circle.

"He is Zeke Culpepper, a hired man and a Freedonian. I paid him to assist me in reclaiming the book."

The elder looked at Zeke. "Do you understand the importance of these books?"

Zeke shook his head. "I can't say that I do."

"The world is changing rapidly," the elder said. "These books and the others will guarantee that this change is meaningful...and peaceful. Your country will play an important part in this change, but now without our help. It is not by chance that you are here, Ezekiel Culpepper."

"Excuse me, elders, but I'm probably the wrong person to

talk to," Zeke replied. "Like Famara said I'm a hired man. I helped him for pay, and I came here for more pay. I'm not one you want to share greater meanings with."

"Perhaps if you saw for yourself you would change your mind," Famara said. He turned his attention to Elders.

"It is forbidden," the female elder said.

"But Elders! Zeke as proven himself in my charge."

"Forbidden," the elder repeated.

Zeke scowled at Famara. "I though you said I'd get paid more gold if I came here with you."

Famara forced a smile. "You will, my friend."

A servant entered the room with a satchel the size of the one holding the books. He came to Zeke then opened it. It was filled with gold.

"Thank you for your help, Ezekiel Culpepper. We wish you well," the elder said. "Accept this gold and this feast as a gesture of our gratitude."

The servants brought in food for the travelers. It was a roasted sheep, stuffed with chicken which in turn was stuffed with eggs. Various bowls fill with rice, sauces and a platter of bread were set beside the meat. Zeke looked at Famara in desperation and Famara laughed.

He pointed at the roasted meat. "That is Mischoui. It takes all day to cook, which means our arrival was expected. That is Assab, millet that you eat with this sauce. The bread is Tadjala. Eat! It is all very good."

Zeke sat beside Famara, mimicking his every move. The food was different yet tasty; in moments he was so stuffed it was hard to stand.

"Was everything to your liking?" Famara asked.

Zeke patted his stomach. "Yes it was. That was some mighty fine eating."

"Excellent! You will stay with me tonight," Famara said. "Tomorrow we will set out for Tripoli."

*   *   *

Famara led Zeke to his home, Amadou following with their possessions. The horro's anxiousness grew with each step. He hoped when he opened the door Kande would be there to greet him. He'd been gone almost a year, more than enough time for Kande to think him dead and to marry another. When he reached the door he hesitated.

"Well, what are you waiting for?" Zeke said.

Famara knocked on the door. He was answered by a squeal from behind him. He turned to see Kande running to him, her baskets sprawled on the ground where she dropped him. In her arms she carried...a child?

Kande walked up to him, a proud smile on her face.

"Famara, meet your daughter," she said.

"My...my daughter?" Famara fell to his knees before his wife, extending his arms. Kande placed the child in his hands then she drew her close, tears streaming from his eyes.

Zeke pushed back his hat then rested his hand on his waist.

"Well I'll be...blessed," he said.

Kande knelt beside him. "It seems our night together before you departed was a blessing for us both."

Famara kissed Kande. "It seems so. What is her name?"

"She has no name," Kande replied. "I could not name her without her father."

"What if something had happened to me?" Famara asked. "What if I didn't come back?"

"The moment I discovered I was pregnant I knew you would return. The ancestors would not have it any other way."

Famara stood carefully. It was then he remembered Zeke.

"Kande, this is Zeke Culpepper. He will be our guest this evening."

Kande studied Zeke then shared a warm smile.

"Hello Zeke," she said.

"Hello ma'am," Zeke said. "It's a pleasure to meet you, but due to circumstances I think it might be better I stayed somewhere else. Looks like you and Mrs. Keita have some serious catching up to do before tomorrow."

Kande's smile faded. "Tomorrow? Famara, what does he mean?"

"Amadou will take you to a hostel. It is a good place." Famara avoided Kande's question. "Most Europeans that visit Timbuktu stay there. It will suit you."

"I'm much obliged to you looking out for me," Zeke said. "I enjoyed that good food we shared with the Elders."

"I think you are Soninke, Zeke Culpepper," Famara said with a smile. "Amadou will arrange food for you as well. I will see you in the morning."

Zeke shook Famara's hand then tipped his hat to Kande.

"Nice meeting you, ma'am." He strolled off with Amadou. Kande smiled until Zeke was out of earshot.

"What does he mean tomorrow, Famara? Where are you going tomorrow?"

Famara regarded Kande's worried face and the oblivious smile of his nameless daughter.

"I'm taking Zeke back to Tripoli. I was hoping..."

"You were hoping what?" Kande asked.

"It's nothing," he said. "Just a notion."

"We will discuss this no longer," Kande decided. "I've had my fill of the Elders' business. Come let's go inside and give our daughter a name. Once she is asleep I will welcome you home properly."

Famara grinned as he took his wife's hand then led her inside their home.

*　　*　　*

The Hotel Ali was located on the west of Timbuktu in a place known as the Foreign Compound. Most of the people walking these streets wore garb familiar to Zeke, though none of them seemed to be Freedonians. He wasn't surprised; most Freedonians didn't give a hoot about the African continent let alone a city as isolated as Timbuktu. President Douglass always included Africa in his speeches, referring to it as the Motherland, the home of all Negro men and women and probably white folks, too. He smiled as he thought about how riled up most white folks got when he said that, especially the Slavers. The president was sure that the future of Freedonia and New Haiti depended on the Motherland. After what Zeke had seen over the past few months he agreed.

Amadou interrupted his musing.

"Sir, everything has been arranged."

He handed Zeke a key.

"Your room is on the first floor. It will be cooler. I instructed the manager to have your food delivered."

"That's mighty kind of you," Zeke answered. He reached into his pocket, extracting a small gold piece as a tip. Amadou shook his head.

"No! No! I serve the Elders. There is no need to pay me. Be brave when the time comes. That is all that we ask."

The young man was on his way before Zeke could ask what he meant by his parting statement. Another boy dressed in a white robe and matching cap took his bags then led him up the narrow stairs then down a dank hallway which led to his room. The boy jiggled the key in the lock before opening it then carried Zeke's belongings inside.

Zeke spent the first part of his day cleaning his weapons. Dust was everywhere in Timbuktu; on the streets, in the air, in his hair and in his food. Still, he could see why Famara was so anxious to get back. With friendly people and a beautiful wife like Kande he was surprised he ever left. But Famara was dedicated to the Elders and the cause. Zeke met men like Famara in during the

Reunion War. It didn't matter if they were Haitian, Freedonian, or American; they had that blind loyalty to their land that made them do unreasonable things. It was one of the reasons why he quit then became a bounty hunter.

He lay back on the hard bed, fell to sleep then dreamed of home. More specifically he dreamed of Pauline. He remembered how he last saw her, the white chemise barely covering her curves, her beautiful face framed by her curly, sweaty hair. The urge to return home flared. He awoke then looked at the gold stuffed satchel beside his bed. What it contained was enough to pay Pierre for the book he wasn't going to bring back, pay off his farm debt and...marry Pauline. If she would have him, of course. They would marry in the church, not that anyone would be surprised. He frowned when he thought of the reverend holding his hand out for a sizable tithe. But he'd have no problem with that, maybe. He'd cross that bridge when he came to it. The excitement of the day crept up on him; a deep yawn escaped his mouth. He closed his eyes and the image of Pauline dressed in his shirt whipping up grits, eggs and bacon came to mind. Now that was a better image to doze off to. Much better.

He awoke to urgent banging at his door.

"Alright, alright!" he said. He opened the door to Amadou's serious face.

"Sir, you must come with me quickly!"

Zeke threw on a pair of pants and a shirt, leaving his side arms behind but grabbing his shotgun. He and the boy ran through the hotel then emerged onto the street to a startling sight. Dozens of armed men sitting on horses waited, with Famara at the lead.

"What's this, Famara?" he asked as he mounted his horse.

"I don't know," Famara replied. "All I know is the Elders called an emergency council requesting all the horro attend."

They rode to the same compound he'd met the elders earlier. When they reached the chamber the elders were seated in their circle. One of the elders stood in the center with one of the book he and Famara had just returned. As soon as the horros settled she reached into the book then extracted a small metal device.

"This is not ours," she said.

"Oh shit....I mean Lord help us," Zeke whispered.

"The Germans have played our own game against us," the woman said. "It is good we found this before we returned the book to Wagadu, otherwise our secret would be no more. It is not good for Timbuktu, however."

The woman gazed across the crowd.

"Famara Keita, Zeke Culpepper. Step forward."

Zeke and Famara made their way through the crowd. Once they reached the elder Famara fell to his knees. Zeke did the same.

"Forgive me Elders. Forgive me brothers. My failure has brought shame and danger to you all. I am willing to do what I must. I'm willing to die for my transgression."

Zeke's eyes went wide. "Now wait just a goddamn minute. I realize we might have screwed up. But begging your pardon I'm not about to take a bullet for it. Not without a fight."

"Famara, stand up," the elder said. "No one is asking for your lives, Ezekiel. Famara, you are one of our finest horros. To lose you because of an error of judgment would be the failure of us all. You know these Germans. You know what they are capable of. So you will plan the defense of Timbuktu while the others deliver the book to its rightful place. You must defend this city at all cost. They must think that Timbuktu is the treasure that they seek."

"I will, elder," Famara answered.

The elder looked at Zeke.

"As for you, Freedonian, you will assist Famara. I don't expect you to do anymore than what you are paid to do, but you will not be paid for this effort. Consider it a chance to make up for a deal gone wrong."

"That sounds fair," Zeke replied.

"Then let us prepare," the elder said. "Babylon is coming. And we will stop it."

34

Dolph marched toward the waiting airships with his elite team, a victorious smile on his face. The generals acted quickly once the decision to retrieve the books was made. The assembled team was from his homeland which insured their loyalty to him. This was obviously Hans doing. The old man was still showing his support. Not only had the generals approved the use of the airships, they also supplied four eisen-kriegers for additional support. The units were modified for desert warfare, fitted with additional cooling vents and circulation fans. Their crews were briefed on the coming mission with the others.

Dolph's eyes narrowed as he spied a group of soldiers gathered before the airships. Had the generals assigned additional troops? If so, they were not necessary. His contacts in North Africa spent their money well, assembling more that enough Tuareg warriors eager to raid Timbuktu for whatever plunder they could seize. His curiosity turned to anger as he recognized the officer among the group: Claus Reuters.

Dolph marched directly to his nemesis.

"What the hell are you doing here? You heard the generals."

Claus smiled. "Good morning to you, Herr field marshal. It's a lovely day to start a mission."

"Answer my question, damn you!"

Claus reached into his pocket, extracting a cigarette. He

took his time lighting it. Claus took a long drag then let the smoke ease from his lips.

"I don't know what they see in you, Dolph. Maybe it's the degrees, the family lineage, I'm not sure. But what I do know is that you are liar and a charlatan. I couldn't stand that show you put on during your hearing, so I waited until the generals were away from your spell to talk some reason into them."

"I see you failed,'" Dolph said.

"Not entirely," Claus said. "I'm coming with you."

Dolph's mouth dropped open. "No!"

Claus reached into his jacket pocket again, this time taking out folded papers.

"My orders," he said.

Dolph snatched the papers from Claus's hand then unfolded them. He read the orders, and then read them again. The bastard had done it. He convinced the general to assign him to the mission.

Dolph pushed the papers into Claus's chest.

"You are here as an advisor only. I suggest you stay out of my way."

"True, I have no authority,' Claus conceded. "But I will file a report. It's time this farce ended."

"The only report you'll file will be one describing my success," Dolph replied. "That is if your report will be factual."

Claus flicked away his cigarette. "I am not liar, field marshal. Besides, there will be no need to fabricate your failure. You'll handle that on your own."

Claus glanced as the approaching soldiers. "My men will be divided among your troops. I will accompany you, of course."

"Keep you distance, Reuters," Dolph snapped. "I don't need your distractions."

He marched away before Claus could respond. It made no difference if the general accompanied them. The outcome would be the same. With Prussian support there was no way they could fail.

The beacon implanted in the book emanated a strong signal and his local forces were ready.

Claus called the troops to attention.

"Men, there has been a change in plans. General Claus Reuters and his team will accompany us on our mission to record our victory to the Reichstag. That being said, I must emphasize his team is here as observers only. They have no authority over our operations no matter their rank. If for any reason any of these men try to issue any orders, ignore them. If they persist report them to me and they will be disciplined immediately. Do you understand?"

Dolph's men shared uncomfortable glances with Reuters's team. Claus glared at him.

"Yes, sir!" the men finally answered in unison.

Dolph smiled. "Good. Everyone proceed to your assigned airship. You'll be briefed once we are aloft."

The men marched away. Claus approached him again.

"Do you think it wise to create tension among fellow soldiers?" he asked between his teeth.

"You created the tension when you arrived on this field," Dolph shot back. "Put it in your report. It will make a nice beginning."

Dolph motioned toward the airship.

"Shall we, general?"

Claus strode by him toward the ship. Dolph followed, his thoughts grim. He would not let Claus Reuters hamper his mission and he was prepared to do anything to make sure he didn't.

The airships were underway within the hour. Dolph inspected the craft making sure his men and their gear were secure before retiring to the ship's compact conference room. He was studying maps of Timbuktu when Claus entered.

"What is your plan, Herr Field Marshall?" he asked.

Dolph looked up at Claus, trying to determine what the general was actually interested in.

He shrugged.

"We'll rendezvous with El Tellak at his stronghold in two days. Together we'll assess Timbuktu's defenses then plan our attack."

Claus frowned. "You're still working with that savage despite his failure to procure the books?"

"He's the only Akedamel in the region with sufficient forces to support our operation. He was also the only one who agreed."

"Not a sound plan in my opinion," Claus replied.

"If you have a better plan I'm interested in hearing it," Dolph said.

Claus sat at the table. "No, Herr Field Marshall. This is your mission. I'm only here as an observer."

"What is it, Claus?" Dolph asked. "Why do you hate me? What have I done to you to warrant your disdain?"

Claus leaned back in his chair. "It's not you personally. It's your kind."

Dolph felt his anger rising. "My kind?"

Claus's eyes narrowed. "Look at you. You have no reason to be in the army. You're a professor for God's sake! The only reason you received a commission is because you're the son of some legacy. You have no military experience; you've never fought in a battle in your life, I suspect. Yet you lead a mission into Africa for your fanciful books and I'm sent along as your babysitter!"

"And I assume you'd do better, Herr General?"

Claus shot to his feet. "Of course I would! I earned this rank, Claus. I'm the son of a cobbler. I enlisted as a private and slogged my way to this position. Along the way I had to deal with the incompetence of men just like you. I watched good soldiers die because of it. Just because a man happened to emerged from the right womb."

"What do you want me to do about it, Claus? I did not make this world. I'm sure some of what you say is true, but incompetence does not discriminate, nor does talent. You believe I shouldn't take advantage of my position? That's illogical. If you were in my position you would do the same."

Claus glared at Dolph. "You should not be here!"

Dolph returned his attention back to his maps. "You've done well for yourself despite your beginnings, Claus. I suggest you focus on that. Don't waste your anger on situations you cannot change. Now unless you have something constructive to add I suggest you leave me to my work."

Claus stormed from the room. Dolph shook his head. Claus would be an annoyance but nothing more. It would be best to avoid him as well as he could until they returned to Prussia.

The thin strip of fertile land near the North African coast quickly gave way to the enormity of the Sahara. The ships glided over miles of sand, scrubs and dunes, a magnificent scene of pastels dotted by the occasional oasis. El Tellak's compound filled the valley of a range of mountains rising from the center of the desert fed by a large oasis. Tents, people and camels surround the large lake.

Dolph stood on the deck of the lead airship with its captain.

"Take us down behind the dunes beyond the oasis," he ordered.

"Yes sir," the captain said.

"Kruger, prepare the men for landfall. We'll set up camp outside the oasis. There will be no fraternization with the Tuaregs, do you understand?"

"Yes, Herr Field Marshall."

The Prussians disembarked then immediately went about setting up camp. Dolph was inspecting their work when the Tuaregs appeared, five camel riders with additional camels following. Dolph signaled Claus and two of his minor officers and they met the riders on the outskirts of their camp. The rider who first spoke to them was a heavily armed woman, her face hidden by a shesh.

"Which one of you is the Prussian Dolph?"

Dolph stepped forward. "I am."

"I am Menna, sister of El Tellak," she said. "You will come

with me."

Dolph and the others began to walk to the camels and the Tuaregs raised their rifles. The Prussians scrambled to their guns.

"Only you," Menna said to Dolph.

Kruger came to his side. "Sir, I would advise against it."

"The Tuaregs are our allies," Dolph said. "I'll be fine."

One of the Tuaregs forced a camel to kneel and Dolph mounted. They rode away from the Prussian camp over the dune to El Tellak's compound. They weaved through the crowded camp to the large tent on the edge of the reservoir. He dismounted then Menna led him to the entrance. The guards checked him for weapons then lifted the flap. El Tellak sat on a mound of silk pillows, flanked by a plain looking woman on his left and an elderly woman on his right.

"Stand here," Menna ordered. She proceeded to El Tellak, taking position behind him. Tellak motioned for Dolph to sit; since there was no pillow for him he sat cross-legged on the sandy surface.

"Welcome to my kel, Field Marshall," Tellak said. "I must say I'm surprised you reached out to me for this mission."

"To be honest you weren't my first choice," Dolph said.

"Failure is not something I encourage."

"I see you value honesty," Tellak said. "The let me be honest as well. None of the other kels took your offer because I threatened to attack them if they did. I lost your book, but the man who caused my failure resides in Timbuktu. It is my intention to capture him then kill him slowly for his insult."

"I have no interest in your vengeance," Dolph said. "The books are my only concern. Are you sure they are in Timbuktu?"

"I'm positive. My spies informed me of their arrival, and Menna confirmed the information."

"Excellent," Dolph stood. "All that's left is to form a plan of attack."

"My men will accompany you to your camp," Tellak said.

"They will discuss plans there with you. I hear you have the steam men with you."

Dolph's eyebrows rose. "How did you know?"

"The Sahara belongs to me, Field Marshall. Nothing escapes my notice. Now go, I tire of this discussion. Rest well, for the next few days will be very exciting, and our sun and heat will take a toll on your pale body."

Dolph nodded. Menna led him out of the tent then to his camel. It was a disrespectful meeting planned merely for El Tellak to establish his superiority. It had no effect on Dolph. His only concern was the books. They were so close to the end of this journey nothing, not even a pompous Tuareg, would distract him. It was time to collect the prize.

35

The morning prayer callers of Timbuktu were not alone in their mud-brick minarets this clear morning. Horros with long range binoculars stood beside them, scanning the horizon in every direction. Outside the city the surrounding desert teemed with additional horros patrolling the dunes in search for the inevitable attack. Even the Niger River miles south was under observation, the fishing boats occupied by horro allies. In a non-descript building in the center of town reports were gathered and analyzed on a large regional map. The blue bars on the map indicated known Tuareg encampments within striking distance of the city; the red, green and white bars indicating European embassies and forces. Although the Elders were certain the Germans were alone on this operation they took nothing for granted.

Zeke stood beside Famara, the two of them joined by a dozen other men surrounding an oblong table. Their cohorts reflected the various people of the Sahel; blue robed Tuaregs, plain dressed and pious Kanuri, cone hat crowned Fulani, brightly colored Hausa, warrior garbed Yoruba, and others added to the richly diverse gathering. Though they were of different people, they all shared one common bond; they were horro pledged to the Elders and sworn to protect the secrets of Wagadu.

Elder Bosso stood in their midst, pointing at the map of Timbuktu and vicinity with a thin stick.

"We have concentrated our forces to the north," he said in

his gravely voice. "This is the most likely approach. Our flanks are well protected. If their attack shifts to either side we can reinforce with cavalry until the main forces respond."

"What about the south?" Zeke asked.

"Why does he speak?" The Hausa glared at Zeke and Famara. "If you two had done your job we wouldn't be here."

Elder Bosso raised his hand. "This is neither the time nor place for such words, Balarabe. We are here to plan strategy, not pick old wounds."

Zeke glanced at Famara and the Hausa. There was apparently no love loss between the two. He'd have to ask his friend about it later.

"The river is the least less likely approach," Elder Bosso continued. "The Germans have no allies south of Timbuktu, nor do the Tuaregs. Still, we do have eyes there, but I'll admit if they attack from the south we would be hard pressed to react."

"It is not critical," Famara said. "The books are on their way to Wagadu. We will hold out long enough to discourage the attack. If they penetrate Timbuktu we will abandon the city."

"Let's hope it doesn't come to that," Elder Bosso said. "Now go. If you all do what you are capable of, today's victory is assured. He raised his hand as if he held a spear.

"Hoooh! Dierra, Agada, Ganna, Silla! Hoooh! Fasa!" he shouted.

"Hoooh! Dierra, Agada, Ganna, Silla! Hoooh! Fasa!" the horro repeated.

The group broke up, each horro returning to his unit and his assigned position.

"Famara, Zeke!" Elder Bosso called out.

The two men approached the elder.

"What do you wish, Elder?" Famara asked.

"Your friend expressed a great concern," the elder said. "I was overconfident in my planning. I should have given more thought to a southern approach. Famara, I would like you and your men to cover the river."

Famara looked skeptical. "Excuse my hesitancy Elder, but is there another reason you wish to insult us by taking us away from the brunt of the fight?"

Elder Bosso smiled. "I know you are a great horro, Famara, and I trust your assessment of your friend's skills. But your presence among the others will cause dissention and we can't afford that at this time. You will have time to answer their concerns later. For now we must be prudent."

"For now," Famara said.

Famara signaled his warriors.

"To your horses."

Zeke studied his friend as they mounted.

"If I were you I'd be relieved," he said.

"You are not me, Freedonian," Famara said.

"Whoa now!" Zeke leaned on his horse's neck. "So we're getting all formal now. Sorry if I offended you."

"You don't understand," Famara replied. "For a horro not to be in the fighting is a dishonor. I should be leading the main defense, not sitting in the rear in reserve."

Zeke pushed back his hat then thought better of it when the bright sunlight hit his eyes. He pushed it back into place.

"I've been in a few battles myself, and believe you me the front is not where you want to be."

Famara glared at him. "This is not about survival! It's about honor!"

"I have a farm and a pretty young lady waiting for me back home," Zeke said. "It's my goal to get back to both of 'em in one piece with your gold. I can deal with living with a little less honor."

"That is where we are different, Zeke." Famara pulled his carbine from its sheath then inspected it as he talked. "Honor above all. If I die in battle defending Wagadu I honor my family and generations to follow."

"I wonder what your pretty wife and beautiful child would

think about that honor," Zeke said.

Famara eyes narrowed. "We will speak no more of this. I feel I will lose much of my respect for you if we do."

Zeke shrugged. "Like I told you before, I'm a bounty hunter. I do the job, I get paid, I go home."

Famara stared at Zeke in a way that made him uncomfortable.

"You are much more than that, Ezekiel Culpepper. The day you realize it your life will change."

They rode though the city to the southern outskirts. Famara raised his hand and the horro halted. Zeke took a head count; there were thirty men total, counting himself and Famara. They were armed with carbines, pistols, knives and...swords. The swords baffled Zeke. He had his machete strapped to his back, but he had no intentions of using it. If anyone got that close to him it was probably time to high tail it. But he got the feeling these horro would rather fight with the swords than guns. It was a nice thought, but that was not about to happen anytime soon.

They positioned themselves in a house owned by the Elders.

"Shouldn't we be a little closer to the river?" Zeke asked.

"No," Famara spoke as he rechecked his rifle. "Our position is easily defended."

"We could hit them harder in the river than here," Zeke said. "They would be packed in boats."

Famara looked up, his face shocked. "That would be dishonorable!"

"It was low down when those folks stole your books," Zeke replied. "The way I see it honor doesn't come into play here."

Famara seemed to consider his words. "We will compromise," he finally said. "If they choose to attack we will ride out to meet them on the banks. You are right. Such men don't deserve the honor we give each other."

They day crept by with no attack. The horros kept vigil

despite the false information they received, refusing to give their attackers any advantages. Their diligence was rewarded. Lights appeared on the horizon shortly after night settled over the city. At first glance they seemed like stars, but they grew in intensity and size with each minute. The horros called out and the warning drums sounded.

Zeke and Famara heads jerked toward the sound to the north. Zeke's stomach fluttered as he kissed his cross then tucked it into his shirt.

"Here we go," he whispered.

Famara stepped out of the house then raised his binoculars to his eyes, scanning the riverbank.

"Nothing so far," he called out. He looked toward the north.

"Airships," he said. "With lights"

A boom cracked the night silence.

"And cannons," Zeke said.

The horro rushed into the open, their rifles at the ready. They looked to the north, the rattle of gunfire and the roar of voices carrying through the empty street. City folk peeked out their doors and windows but dared not come into the street. Very few evacuated despite plenty of warning of the attack. They trusted the horros' skills.

Zeke watched Famara pace, his hands working his rifle.

"This is outrageous!" he shouted.

The other horro stood around him now, their expressions revealing their intentions. Famara looked at them then to Zeke.

"Enough of this," he barked. "Let's..."

They were doused with blinding light.

"Take cover!" Zeke shouted.

Bullets riddled the area, puffs of dust marking their strikes. Horro fell dead and wounded into the streets while others dove for safety inside the nearest buildings. Zeke managed to look up before ducking for cover. A Prussian airship emerged from the light like a death demon. The gunfire from the airship was relentless.

Zeke and Famara sat side by side, the building around them falling apart to the gunfire.

Zeke snatched his shotgun from his leg. He twisted the barrel free then opened the satchel he'd salvaged from his dead horse. Inside was an extended barrel which he screwed onto the shotgun. He reached into the bag again, taking out a stock extension. He clamped it onto the gun.

Zeke looked at Famara then winked and nodded.

"Always be prepared," he said.

He loaded the shotgun with explosive shells. The gunfire paused as the airship gunners reloaded. Zeke jumped into the open then fired two shots toward the lights. The shells exploded seconds later and the sky erupted with burning hydrogen. The brilliant light from the blast revealed another secret; Prussian soldiers running toward the city from the river, supported by four lumbering mechanical men.

"Looks like you got your fight!" Zeke shouted.

Famara looked at him, a wide grin on his face.

"Excellent!" he shouted back.

The horro fired into the darkness at the advancing Prussians. From the walls, more horro shot flaming arrows into the sand, illuminating the attacking Prussians. The mechanical men opened fired, raking the ramparts. Zeke sprinted to the ramparts with his modified shotgun, Famara close behind. No words needed to be exchanged between the two. As they reached the ramparts Famara scooped up a bow and a quiver of arrows from a fallen archer. The two squatted as Famara lit an arrow then nocked the bow. They sprang up together, spotting the closest metal man only a few yards away from the city. Famara released the arrow; it struck the mechanical man where the head unit joined the body. Zeke shot two explosive rounds into the head unit; they detonated, blowing the unit free and ejecting the operators into the air then onto the sands.

They were on the move before the explosion settled, their previous position strafed with gunfire. The second metal man went up in flames as well from their coordinated attack. The third metal man fell still as its operators abandoned it. A yell rose from below them as the horro charged into the Prussians, side arms and swords drawn. Famara threw the bow and arrows to the ground then drew his saber.

"Come, Zeke!" he said. "Now we fight like men!"

Zeke extracted his machete from its back sheath.

"I'm right behind you, partner!"

"Famara! Famara!"

Zeke and Famara looked toward the north of the city. A horro rode down the street toward them, a look of terror on his face. The duo hurried down the steps and met the rider.

"Famara, the Tuaregs have broken through! They are in the city!"

Famara looked at Zeke.

"I must help," he said. "You must lead in my place."

"Famara, I'm not sure..."

Famara grasped Zeke's shoulders. "This is no time for your indecision Ezekiel Culpepper. Can I depend on you?"

Zeke nodded.

"Good!"

Famara ran to the nearest horse then climbed into the saddle. He galloped away with the horro.

"Now ain't this something," Zeke said. He waved his machete over his head.

"Hoooh Fasa!" he shouted, and then charged out with the horro.

36

Dolph cursed as the second eisen-krieger exploded. What he thought would be an advantage had become a death trap. The savages had been warned of the attack; there was no doubt in his mind. Two airships had been shot down north of the city; the airship supporting them was down as well. Despite their losses the Tuaregs were holding against the city defenders even though they had yet to enter the city. The heated fighting in the north drew most of the horro forces there but apparently not all.

"Shut this thing down!" he shouted to the drivers.

"We're almost to the city, Herr Field Marshal," the driver replied.

"Didn't you see what just happened to the other Eisen-krieger?" he shouted. "We're sitting ducks in this thing!"

The driver turned to face him, an annoyed look on his face.

"Sir, our Eisen-krieger is better armed than the others. It's..."

A loud ping interrupted the driver's speech. Dolph braced for what he knew would follow. There was a louder ping, then an explosion that deafened him. The eisen-krieger careened to the left, stumbling like a drunkard. The driver fought with the controls, eventually steadying the vehicle.

"See sir," he said with a smile. "Tough as diamonds!"

The second explosion filled the cabin with fire. Dolph

watched in horror as flames consumed the driver and gunner. He regained his senses then kicked the rear hatch open. He scrambled from the passenger hatch then clambered down the teetering Eisen-krieger until he was low enough to jump. He landed hard on the sand, rolling to his feet them limping away as the Eisen-krieger fell backwards, shaking the ground as it struck. Dolph did a self inspection. He was unhurt. His side arm was still with him, as was his sword. A grim laugh escaped his lips; he'd brought the sword so he could raise it in triumph as they marched through Timbuktu. That was apparently not to be. Still, there was the matter of the books. If he could get to them he would accomplish his primary goal.

The horro charged from the city, waving there sabers over their heads. A dozen fell to the volley from the advancing Prussians but the others reached the Prussians before they could fire another round. Dolph locked his eyes on the city. If he could get inside he could follow the map leading to where the books were kept. He skirted the melee before him, trying to sneak unnoticed into the city. He was almost there when he saw a familiar person running toward him.

"Freedonian!" he spat.

He pulled his pistol then fired. The Freedonian was already moving as he extracted his own side arm and fired back. The two exchange fire as they dodged back and forth seeking cover. Dolph's gun clicked; he was empty. He was reaching for an extra clip when he saw the Freedonian rushing him, his machete drawn. A exultant smile came to Dolph's face as he drew his sword. He took a fencing stance.

"So this is how you wish to die, Freedonian," he said.

"I wouldn't get ahead of myself," the Freedonian replied.

The Freedonian took a stance as well, his machete held forward, his left hand tucked behind his back.

"A little thing I learned in New Haiti," the Freedonian said.

Dolph attacked. His swordplay was precise and furious, but somehow the Freedonian block his every thrust and slash. The man fought oddly, crouched low and continuously moving in a dance-like motion. Dolph winced as the Freedonian cut him across the thigh. He retaliated with a slash that ripped the Freedonian's sleeve but drew no blood. The Freedonian swept his short fat blade at Dolph's feet; Dolph hopped over the blade into a solid punch to his face. The blow stunned him, knocking him onto his back. He held onto his sword, swinging wildly to keep the Freedonian away while he regained his feet. When he stood he bled from a gash across his chest.

The Freedonian stood before him, weaving and feinting. Dolph stumbled, his strength flowing away with his blood. Still, he held his stance. There would be no surrender.

A shower of bullets splattered around the Freedonian. The man rolled away, seeking cover from the metal deluge.

"Eriksson!"

His name came from above. Dolph looked up to see the airship hovering over him like an armed cloud. A rope ladder fell before him. He dropped his sword then grabbed the lowest rung. He climbed, gritting his teeth as he rose higher and higher. As he reached the top he met the face of Claus. Dolph reluctantly took the man's hand and Claus pulled him inside.

"Why did you save me?" he said.

"I may not like you, but you're a Prussian officer," Claus replied. "I won't let you die among these savages."

Two of Claus's men treated Dolph's wounds as Claus stood over him.

"I'm taking you back to Prussia to answer to your failure," Claus said.

Dolph grinned. "I see the old Claus has returned."

"I will tell the tribunal of your valiant effort to secure the books," Claus said. "You're a fool, but you're a courageous fool."

Dolph was about to reply when he heard a loud pop. The

color drained from his face.

"I don't think either of us will get the chance to say much else," Dolph said.

The airship burst into flames.

Zeke lowered the shotgun from his shoulder, watching the burning airship tumble into the horizon like the setting sun.

"Gotcha," he said.

He limped back to Timbuktu, shotgun tucked under his arm.

37

Famara and Ousmane maneuvered their horses through the fleeing inhabitants toward the north. The sound of desperate struggle amplified with each moment; soon it filled his ears. The Prussians and Tuaregs had breached the perimeter defenses. Prussian airships burned in the distance but had apparently survived long enough to use their aerial firepower with effective results. His brothers succumbed to their warrior instincts, preferring individual battle to organized resistance.

"Do you have knives?" Famara shouted.

"Yes!" Ousmane answered.

"We'll take out the metal men first," Famara said. "Once their down we'll pull back and set up a firing line."

Ousmane nodded. Both men steered their mounts left toward the closest kreiger. The leviathan twisted at the waist, strafing the sand with its automatic guns and scattering horro whenever they attempted to gather. The Tuaregs raced about on their camels and horses, adding confusion to the scene. Famara pulled up his horse then reached into his knife bag. He slammed a knife hilt against his saddle then threw the knife hard. The primed weapon lodged into the neck piece of the automaton then exploded, blasting the headpiece from the body. A cheer rose from the beleaguered horros as the Kreiger teetered then collapsed into the sand. A Prussian crawled free of the wreckage before it exploded again. No sooner did he climb to his feet was he cut down by horro gunfire.

The duo rode to the second Kreiger without hesitation. The machine sprinted toward them, guns spitting bullets as it trampled anyone or anything it its path. A cry to his right caused Famara to look; he grimaced as he watched Ousmane roll off his horse, his chest riddled with bullets. He guided his horse right, then left, then right again, dodging the bullet stream aimed at him as he advanced closer and closer to the metal giant. He was almost in range when his horse bucked, sending him flying through the air then landing hard on his left side. His arm took the brunt of the blow; when he scrambled to his feet it hung limp at his side, numb from the impact. A Tuareg on a towering white camel charged toward him, revolver in one hand, takouba raised in the other. Famara recognized his face in an instant.

"El Tellak!"

He ran toward the vile man, snatching a throwing knife from his bag. He hit the hilt against his hip in stride then hurled the knife into the camel's breast. El Tellak's shocked face disappeared as the knife exploded, filling the air with blood, smoke and flesh. The force of the explosion knocked Famara off his feet and onto his back. He grimaced as he stood, intending to finish the kreiger still wreaking havoc among his brethren. Instead El Tellak strode toward him; his robes tattered, his wounds healing with each step.

"Did you think it would be that easy, horro?" El Tellak spat.

"You killed me once. Now it's my turn to kill you!"

Famara didn't have time to wonder why the Tuareg still lived. Tellak fell on him with fury and skill, his takouba slicing and stabbing at him like a serpent. Famara met the attack with equal skill, parrying and dodging despite his numbed left side. Tellak raised his revolver but Famara kicked it from his hand then drew his leg back before Tellak could sever his foot. The tip of Famara's saber kissed Tellak's cheek, causing the man to twist his head away to save his jaw. The wound bled for a moment then healed before Famara's eyes. The horro cursed as Tellak grinned.

They clashed again, the battle raging around them. The horros, inspired by Famara's presence, rallied in the ruins of the nearby buildings. A blast caught both men's attention, their heads jerking toward the sound. The horros managed to find an old cannon among the city's caverns and put it to effective use. The Eisen-krieger reeled, a massive dent in its breastplate. The horros hurried to load the cannon again as the Eisen-krieger and Tuaregs surged toward their position. They were met by a deadly fusillade from horro rifles.

Famara took advantage of the distraction. He kicked Tellak's right knee then chopped hard with his saber, severing Tellak's left hand. The man screamed out then staggered back. He glared at the bleeding stump as it slowly healed. Though seriously wounded, his energy was unabated. He lunged at Famara, who spun to his left then plunged his saber into Tellak's back. Tellak managed to push away from Famara, twisting and striking out with his sword as he fell away. The blade ripped Famara's shirt then gashed his chest.

The horro was undeterred. He chased Tellak, stabbing him over and over; trying to overwhelm the man's mysterious healing powers. He was so engrossed in his task he almost saw the dagger streaking toward him too late. He fell back awkwardly as the poisoned blade flew by.

"Menna!" Tellak shouted.

A robed figure jumped between the adversaries. Menna crouched, a dagger in her right hand, takouba in her left. Famara advanced slowly on the woman.

"Kill him!" Tellak shouted.

Menna looked at her wounded brother then looked at the man she'd hunted across half the world. Her eyes narrowed then she stepped aside, sheathing her sword and dagger.

"Menna?" A shocked look ruled Tellak's face.

The woman stared at Famara, nodded then turned her back. Famara leaped at Tellak, swinging his saber with both hands wrapped tight around the hilt. Tellak was still staring at the woman when Famara cut off his head. It fell into the sand with a soft thud. Famara held his sword in guard position as the woman slowly turned to face him. Instead of going for her weapons, she raised her hands. Famara stepped away as the woman reached into her robes then took out a canvas sack. She picked up Tellak's head, raising it slowly to study it face to face. Then he held it high then let out a piercing cry. The Tuaregs looked toward her. They returned the cry, some of the voices cracking with sorrow. Then they retreated, mounting their camels then riding out of Timbuktu. The woman placed Tellak's head into the sack then secured it to her waist belt. She backed away from Famara to her camel which knelt as she mounted.

"Hut hut!" she said. The camel rose to its feet. She yanked the reins and the beast turned toward the north, following its brethren from the city.

Famara watched the Tuaregs withdrawal. The Prussians fled as well. With their eisen-kriegers and airships destroyed and the Tuaregs retreating they were vastly outnumbered. The horros waved their sword and fired their guns in celebration. Famara's eyes stayed on the horizon. Wherever El Tellak hid, his people were in for a surprise. There would be a new Akedamel, one the Soninke was sure he would meet again.

38

Zeke moseyed through the streets of Timbuktu, nodding to his left and right at the joyous residents. He found Famara sitting in the street near the northern gate, a healer busy bandaging his wounds. The horro looked up then shared a triumphant smile.

"We have won!" Famara shouted.

"Seems like it," Zeke replied. He regarded the carnage around him and his stomach became queasy. It was a sight he hoped he'd never see again despite his chosen profession. Hunting a man down was one thing; violence could be avoided most of the time. But war? He'd seen enough of it. Images of Pauline and his farm emerged in his head, calming his mind.

"It's time I went home, Famara," he said. "I've done my part. Just give me my money and I'll be on my way."

"I understand, my friend," Famara answered. "But there is one more thing I would ask of you."

Zeke shook his head. "No. No more killing. I've had enough of it for a while."

"It doesn't involve the taking of life," Famara said. "As a matter of fact, it's quite the opposite."

The healer completed his work then began inspecting Zeke. Famara came to his feet then dropped his hands on Zeke's shoulders.

"Let us savor our victory then rest. Tomorrow we will discuss things further."

Zeke made his way to his hotel room accompanied by the healer. The building escaped major damage but the road leading to it was littered with debris. The healer followed him to his room then dressed his wounds. Once he was comfortable the healer gave him a tea that made him feel especially good and infinitely relaxed. Sleep came almost immediately; when he awoke with the morning prayer call he felt refreshed and energetic. It was when he attempted to sit up that he was reminded of his wounds.

A tapping at his door caught his attention.

"Come in."

A valet dressed western style entered his room with a tray of food and drink. He sat the tray on the nightstand next to the bed.

"Famara waits for you in the lobby," the valet informed him.

"Thank you," Zeke replied. He reached into his pocket for a tip but the man shook his head.

"The Elders have seen to it. Have a nice day, Freedonian."

"Zeke. My name is Zeke."

The valet grinned. "Have a nice day, Zeke."

Zeke took his time, savoring the delicious meal. Afterwards he washed up then dressed as fast as his wounds allowed.

Famara was standing when he hobbled into the hotel lobby.

"My brother!" he said. "Good morning!"

"You seem mighty spry after fighting all night," Zeke replied.

"It is a wonderful day. My family is safe and the books are secure. Now come, we mustn't waste time."

Two horses waited outside. Zeke wasn't looking forward to the ride in his condition but he had no choice. Luckily their destination wasn't far; the building which held the Elders' council room. When Zeke and Famara entered they were greeted by not only the Elders, but by as many horro that could fit in the small space.

"Elders and brothers!" Famara announced. "Last night we defended our city and our heritage from those who would abuse it for their own purposes. One among us was not of our ranks, but he fought with us with a spirit that would make his ancestors proud."

"What's going on here, Famara?" Zeke whispered.

Famara smiled then stepped away. Elder Bosso broke away from the Elder's circle and took his place.

"Your skills are equal to any horro in this room," the elder said. "Yet you claim to be a bounty hunter, a hired gun. Anyone can see you are more than this."

Zeke pushed back his hat.

"Not to be rude or anything Elder, but I'm the kind of person that likes to get to the point," Zeke said. "What are y'all trying to ask me?"

"We'd like you to become a horro."

Zeke whistled. "That's a mighty fine offer, and believe me I'm honored. You got a fine organization here. But I'm going to have to turn you down. I'm not one for movements. I like to keep it simple."

Elder Bosso took on a confused look. He glared at Famara then returned to the circle. The horro grumbled, making Zeke uneasy.

Famara placed his hand on Zeke's shoulder.

"Maybe if you were to see what we fight for you would decide otherwise."

A roar of protest swept the room.

"It is forbidden!"

"Only those who serve see!"

"The children of Wagadu must protect it."

Famara waited for the protests to subside.

"Look at him," he said. "The blood of Wagadu runs through his veins. Dierra, Agada, Ganna, Silla is his heritage as well."

"Hooh, Fasa!" everyone chanted.

"Though we have bee separated by miles and years, we still

come from the same roots. He has the right to protect Wagadu."

Zeke leaned close to Famara.

"Look Famara, I appreciate what you're doing but my answer is still no," Zeke whispered. "Just give me my pay and I'll be off."

"Suffer me one more day, my friend," Famara said. "Come with us to Wagadu. If after your visit you are still unconvinced I will do as you ask."

"Fair enough," Zeke said.

Famara approached the Elders.

"With your permission I will take Zeke to Wagadu."

"You believe in him this much?" Elder Bosso asked.

"Yes."

The Elders glanced at one another before Bosso answered.

"You have our permission," Elder Bosso said. "But you are responsible for him. If for any reason your friend causes trouble you both will suffer the consequences."

Famara grinned. "Thank you, Elders!"

He strode back to Zeke.

"You're taking quite a risk for me," Zeke said.

"There is no risk, Ezekiel Culpepper. You are a good man." Famara slapped Zeke hard on the back.

"Rest well tonight, brother. Tomorrow we travel to Wagadu!"

* * *

The next morning they set out for Wagadu. To Zeke's dismay they rode camels, which smelled as terrible as they behaved. Despite that they covered the open desert quickly, travelling for two days through scrub brush and sand. The horro were well prepared for the journey with ample provisions. Most of the time they rode the camels, but for long expanses they walked, leading the stubborn beasts along. On the third day they crested a small hill then found themselves looking down onto a valley of dunes.

"We are here," Famara announced.

"This is Wagadu?" Zeke asked. "A bunch of sand hills?"

Their camels knelt and both men dismounted. They walked to the edge of the hill. Famara reached into his robes, extracting a pair of green tinted goggles.

"Put these on," he said.

Zeke put on the goggles.

"Lord have mercy!" he exclaimed.

The dunes became transparent, revealing majestic stone structures beneath them.

"It's a buried city!"

"And so it shall remain until it is time," Famara said. "The sheets of the books are blueprints, designs that operate thousands of machines in Wagadu. The Prussians sought to use the sheets themselves because they don't have the knowledge to duplicate them as they were meant."

"But they would eventually figure it out," Zeke surmised.

"Yes. This is why we had to destroy everything in Dolph's castle."

"So what does Freedonia have to do with all this?"

"Freedonian scientists are close to discovering what we possess on their own. Dr. Carver's work is brilliant. There will come a time when we can combine our knowledge for the good of the world."

"Seems to me you should be talking to Annette and Scofield's folks," Zeke said.

"Annette and Mr. Scofield are loyal to Freedonia. We need someone in Freedonia loyal to us."

Zeke rubbed his chin. "Not much loyalty in a hired man."

"You're more than that," Famara replied. "You could have walked away at any point but you didn't. You risked your life for me and the books. You are a good, loyal man."

"That's what I'd like to believe," Zeke said. "So what do I

have to do?"

"Work for us when we ask," Famara said. "You will be compensated of course. We don't want you chasing a bounty when we need your services."

"And you'll pay off my farm?"

Famara sighed. "Yes Zeke, we'll pay off your farm."

Zeke rubbed his chin. I'm still not sure about this."

"Come," Famara said. "There is much more inside."

Zeke, Famara and the horro walked down the dune, leaving their camels behind. As they approached, the central dune shimmered then revealed a large black door.

"What was that?" Zeke asked.

"Mirage projection," Famara answered. "From a distance it seems there is nothing but dunes. The projector creates the illusion of sand."

"Wagadu technology?"

Famara smiled. "Yes."

The dune echoed with the sound of opening locks then the door slid open. A horro armed with a carbine waved them inside. They entered a lighted corridor, the walls painted in hieroglyphics. The symbols were similar to those in Egypt, yet different.

"I know what you're thinking," Famara said. "It's our belief that Wagadu existed either in synch with Kemet or preceded it. This desert was once grassland and the domain of Wagadu. We think that as the grasslands transformed into desert its people migrated in all directions, taking some but not all of their knowledge with them. A few remained and eventually became the Soninke. But even they lost the great knowledge of Wagadu. It has taken centuries to reclaim, but we are very close."

The rhythmic pulse of working machinery drifted up the corridor as they neared the next portal. Zeke followed Famara through then stopped, stunned by the scene before him. Wagadu was an underground city, with wide avenues emanating like spokes from a central zone of large palatial buildings. The avenues were packed with steam powered vehicles; cars, trucks, wagons and even mechanical men that dwarfed those of Prussia and Freedonia. Zeke saw something zip across his field of vision. He dismissed it, thinking it was a bug or something. Then he saw it again. It was some type of flying vehicle, a contraption different than anything he'd ever seen, even the Freedonian cyclo gyros. When he looked at Famara the horro seemed embarrassed.

"So you were faking when you said you'd never flown," Zeke said.

"No I wasn't," Famara replied. "I have never flown, but I am very familiar with flying craft, even your cyclo gyro."

"I've seen enough," Zeke replied. "Where do I sign?"

"Your word is good enough, my brother," Famara said. "We will return to Timbuktu so the Elders can handle the details."

Famara hugged Zeke, catching him off guard.

"Thank you, Zeke," he said. "You won't regret this."

They exited the building, leaving the wonders of Wagadu behind. Famara trudged back to the camels. Zeke lingered for a few moments longer, rubbing his cross as he gazed at the wonders of Wagadu.

"Lord, you've taken me to a lot of places, but this has got to be the most special," he said. "Give me the strength to hold up my end of the bargain. I sure don't want to let these good folks down. Amen."

He shifted his hat then followed Famara. Together they began the journey back to Timbuktu.

39

The Moroccan airship eased next to the Atlanta Airfield docking tower at midday. The passengers peered out the brass portholes, waiting until the stewards gave the signal for them to proceed to the exits. The ship jerked as the grappling ropes took hold and the passengers bustled about gathering their belongings. The steward, a thin, bronze-skinned man wearing a crisp white uniform punctuated with a red fez with a golden tassel stood in the narrow aisle then flashed a pleasant smile.

"Welcome to Atlanta, jewel of Freedonia," he said. "Please proceed to the exit in an orderly fashion. We hope your journey has been pleasant."

Zeke lifted his head then pushed back his hat, waiting until everyone exited. He wasn't going to rush; he would savor every moment of his arrival home. After claiming his bags he took his time descending the stairs to the terminal. The last time he was in this terminal he pursued a man who had become his friend and employer. It was a strange twist, but one he was grateful for.

To his surprise his steam car was still where he left it, albeit a bit worse for wear. He decided to clean it later. He bothered a nearby worker for a bucket of water, filled the tank then lit the boiler. By the time he loaded the car and completed the inspection the car hissed its readiness. His first instinct was to go home, but he had some business to take care of first.

Zeke sauntered up the flower bordered walkway leading

to Pierre's porch. The warm spring day was complemented by a gentle breeze which kept the heat at bay. He removed his flat cap as he approached then rapped the silver knocker against the oak door.

The door creaked opened, revealing a petite maid with caramel skin and questioning eyes.

"Yes, monsieur?" she said.

"I'm Zeke Culpepper. I'm here to see Pierre."

"Just a minute, monsieur. Please come inside while I inform Monsieur LaRue of your presence."

Zeke stepped inside as he took off his hat. He eased into the plush visitor's chair then settled into the comfortable cushions. The maid glided away to Pierre's sitting room. Moments later the house erupted in shouting.

"Zeke Culpepper! Ce salaud a un sacré culot!"

Zeke grinned as Pierre stormed through house then into to foyer.

"It's been eight months, Zeke. Eight months! You better have my book or my money!"

"I don't have your book or your money," Zeke said.

Pierre's eye bulged. "What? What?"

Zeke stood then grasped his belt. "Seems as though the man who stole that book from you was the original owner. So after I tracked him down he convinced me to let him keep it."

"I don't care who that book belong to! I bought it fair and square!"

Zeke stood and reached into his pocket. Pierre's eyes went wide and he backed away. Zeke took out a small pouch.

"Seeing as though you're out of a book and I did fail to fulfill my duty I brought you a small gift."

Pierre snatched the pouch from his hand and opened it.

"No trinket is going to...Oh mon dieu!"

Pierre took out a huge diamond broach.

"Thought you'd say that," Zeke said. "Think that makes us even. Now if you'll excuse me, I have to get back to my farm."

Zeke didn't wait for Pierre's mouth to close. He strolled back to his steam car then drove away. As he weaved through the roads of Atlanta and into the countryside he patted his chest. Inside his jacket was the deed to his farm. He could finally hang up his guns and take a serious stab at being a farmer.

He reached his farm about dusk. He expected the land to be covered with weeds but instead it looked well groomed. A smile came to his face as he thought of who was responsible.

He unlocked the door then set his down his things. The house was stale from being shut for so long, so he worked his way from room to room opening windows. Afterwards he went out the back door to the barn. Everything was as he left it; his reloader resting on the table, the various custom shotgun shells strewn about.

"Good to be home," he whispered. As he walked back to the house he spied Pauline riding up in her wagon. He walked around his homestead and met her at the gate.

"Welcome home, stranger." The smile on her face warmed his heart.

"Thank you, Miss Pauline. You sure got here fast."

Zeke helped Pauline out of the wagon. She reached into the bed and took out a basket smelling of fried chicken, collards and other home cooked goodness.

"That contraption of yours makes more noise than an army," she said. "I figured you'd be hungry whenever you got back so I brought dinner."

"Now that's what I call a homecoming," Zeke replied.

They walked side by side together to the porch.

"You been gone a long time, Zeke," she said. "I missed you."

"I missed you, too," Zeke replied. "I won't be travelling anytime soon."

"Where did you go?" she asked.

Zeke smiled. "From here to Timbuktu."

Pauline laughed. "Ain't no such place as Timbuktu. That's just a saying."

"Now that's where you you're wrong," Zeke said. "There is a Timbuktu; and I've been there."

They climbed the porch and Zeke opened the door.

"You know I don't believe you," Pauline said.

"Well, come on inside and let me tell you a story," he said.

Pauline gave him a sly grin then entered the house. Zeke followed then closed the door behind them.

End